LAVA, LAVA EVERYWHERE!

There was no time to swear. Icehall twisted around in his headlong plunge and aimed his right arm where he thought the side of the castle was. He clenched his fist hard, and *pfrroww!* went the Black Widow Worker Autoretrieval Device. He heard the adhesive capsule impact close by, felt the cord go taut… then felt the cord snap back at him. The adhesive had failed.

With a grim breath Icehall realized that he had used one cartridge already, in demonstrating the device during the welcome feast. Down below was molten red-orange doom. He clenched his fist again to trigger the last cartridge. *Pfffffrroww-thwackkk!* The roiling lava was scant meters below him.

"Ufff!" he puffed as the cord went taut—and held. He spun wildly around an axis through his navel, and heard all three refrigeration units in the Rabinowicz suit energize at once. Everywhere around him was an orange-yellow glare upon whipping clouds of gas. The side of the castle was nowhere in sight. Icehall was swinging out over the molten rock like a plumb bob. He reached the extreme point of his trajectory, then began swinging back and down. Icehall craned his neck to see where he was heading, and screamed.

The low point of his swing was easily two meters under the surface of the lava.

FIREJAMMER

FIREJAMMER

JEFF DUNTEMANN

Copperwood Press • Scottsdale, Arizona
2019

FIREJAMMER

Copyright © 2019 by Jeff Duntemann. All Rights Reserved
ISBN-13: 978-1-932084-11-5

Cover illustration by Augusta Scarlett.
https://www.scarlettebooks.com/

COPPERWOOD MEDIA, LLC

SCOTTSDALE, ARIZONA

To the eternal memory of and in tribute to
John Keith Laumer 1925-1993
who taught us all how funny aliens were done.

1.

ABOARD STARSHIP
RICHARD M. NIXON

Shuttle *J. Edgar Hoover* was fueled and ready to go. Starship Mechanic First Class Vincent Icehall clung to a hole in a perforated beam with his little finger and checked the readings again. Behind him floated Astrogator Haatchtekfaaz, with one boneless leg coiled around a stanchion and a sour look on his face.

"Call me fussy," the Atrinite said. "Call me nervous. Call me a senile old water-skatch with one eye stuck permanently over my shoulder. This whole thing smells funny."

"Relax, Haatch." Icehall watched the fueling tube retract with a wheeze into its cylinder.

"Relax? You saw the reports Custiss beamed back. All in that funny, stuffy language of his, but I can read under the words, I can! 'The input to their digestive system consists of rocks and organic debris, and the output is epoxy glue.' Weird, I say!"

Icehall shrugged. "Weird is relative. On board *Nixon* our input is epoxy glue, and we output rocks. Weird?"

Haatchtekfaaz grimaced. He grabbed Icehall by one arm and spun him around. "With four eyes open I tell you, I am afraid!" The Atrinite forced his night-eyes wide. Icehall saw his own face reflected in those ghostly, fluid pupils. It was unnerving. He squeezed a cartilaginous shoulder and smiled.

"We'll be okay. I've got friends."

"Friends, he says. I'll loan you a better friend." The Atrinite dug under his silver shipsuit and pressed a small object into Icehall's hand. It was a three-shot pocket tracton with a carved jade handle. All three pips glowed hot green when Icehall thumbed the safety. Icehall shook his head and tucked the weapon back in Haatchtekfaaz's pocket.

"No way. I could get canned for toting on a diplomatic mission. You'll be up here. If we get in trouble, we'll call you, and then you can come running. Deal?"

The Atrinite muttered something in his own language. Then: "What can I say? That's my job. Get out of here now, and come back soon so I can get some sleep!"

Icehall cuffed the astrogator lightly and toed his way down the corridor to the lock. Boddkluskew, the negotiating trade officer of the mission to Scattershot, was hanging over the port. He seemed puzzled as to why he was not falling into the shuttle.

"Peace and somnolent fates, youngster; I regret my old frame won't budge through our passageway. It has been written upon the Nineteen Stones…"

"You go head first, Bod. No, here, wait, we're going to miss my approach window in ten minutes!" Icehall wriggled past the old Phelgre and dove into the shuttle port. Moments later he reached an arm through the port and hauled the tripedal being into the shuttle feet-first. It was tight around Boddkluskew's massive pelvic girdle, but Icehall had gotten him aboard through the same port.

"Icehall, heads up! Where you have been! We're long overdue!" The Captain was struggling with his crash webbing. Papers from his notes were drifting around the cabin.

Icehall reached out a hand and twisted the crashweb buckle the proper way around. The web snapped into position and pulled the Captain flat into the cot. Icehall oriented Boddkluskew in mid air, put one hand on each massive shoulder, and plugged the Phelgre into his species-specific cot as though he were a circuit module.

He then spent a few freeform moments gathering the Captain's wayward notes. The Captain took them with a nod of thanks, then immediately began waving them around. "Duties being what they are, I've only just now had the time to read Mr. Custiss's report. He says that the, er…*Rockchomper* you befriended—must we call them that?"

"You couldn't pronounce what they call themselves, Sir."

"Perhaps. But it has no, well, *dignity*. Doesn't anyone sell a transliteration app? The…*native*…you befriended when you dropped Mr. Custiss here last trip seems to be the local equivalent of court jester, town drunk, and village idiot rolled into one. I'm not sure my crew should be associating with such lowlifes."

Icehall smiled. "I can't drink what he drinks, I can't swear like he swears, and I certainly can't repeat his jokes. Look at it this way—maybe I can make him mend his ways and become a model citizen. Could it hurt to try, Sir?"

The Captain looked away. "Hummmph. Eating rocks! Indeed!"

Icehall secured the hatch and settled himself into the forward command cot. The shuttle came to quick life with a sound of fans and idling fusion tube.

"Take us down, Mr. Icehall," directed the Captain.

"Have pity on my old bones," said Boddkluskew.

Icehall forced a grin at the bulkhead and blew them free of the *Nixon* with a lurch.

2.

SCATTERSHOT LANDFALL

Icehall muttered a lot going down. Scattershot was a tough planet to orbit properly, with sixteen near-planetary bodies within a million-kilometer radius to make things interesting. The configuration was stable, but *not* simple. Furthermore, he had to land the shuttle atop a castle in a deep valley between mountain range that made the Himalayas look middling.

Not to worry; he had done it all before. Icehall had a rapport with his shuttles that bordered on transhuman. He made the approach window, crewmembers notwithstanding, and even after two years, it was all coming back. Beneath a smoky veil of atmosphere, Scattershot was craggy and colorful. Long, finger-shaped seas threaded between young, heavily-volcanic mountain ranges. The constant outgassing from thousands of active volcanoes prevented the atmosphere from being breathable by creatures used to simple oxygen-nitrogen mixes. Too much sulfur dioxide, too much carbon monoxide and dioxide, too many oxides of nitrogen. Once the planet's tectonics settled down a little the atmosphere would clean itself up in a few million years. But with sixteen moons the size of Luna or larger, Scattershot's plates would be a long time settling down.

The tight spiral in from high orbit had been carefully planned. Once Icehall saw the deep gash between needle peaks creeping over the horizon, it was an easy drop in. Six of Scattershot's monster moons spread considerable light across the valley. Custiss's beacon sang an unmistakable polyphonic song in their ears as Icehall throttled back and began their vertical descent.

There were many castles in Castle Valley. Icehall could spot several of them in the ruddy moonlight. They were of varying sizes, though all seemed enormous, and all were roughly similar in shape: inverted elliptical mushroom caps with a sculpted stem rising from the middle. Castle Alpha was one of the largest.

"Isn't it rude to land atop their castle?" Boddkluskew asked. "I suspect we put out considerable flame."

"No flame at all—just good, clean plasma. Tomorrow morning you'll see why, Bodd. It's the only really flat place for hundreds of miles."

"But the Rockchompers…"

"They have asbestos hides."

"Indeed…"

"Would I lie to you?"

The old Phelgre made the Sign of the Two Broken Stones, and looked the other way.

"Less banter, Mr. Icehall," said the Captain. "I would prefer you concentrate on an effective landing." The Captain's knuckles were white.

"Yessir…any second now…*mark!*"

Icehall's hand twitched on the throttle, and J. *Edgar Hoover* dropped a meter or two for the Captain's benefit. With the Captain relaxed, Icehall made the final fifty meters and touched down without a bump.

The Captain was out of his cot and stretching his legs even before the shuttle's landing pads touched stone. "Mr. Icehall, I have received a strong recommendation from Dr. Custiss that we lower the shuttle down on its ventral skids. He says that local earthquake activity being what it is that that would be safer. See to it."

"Yessir." Through the plates Icehall saw artificial light approaching the shuttle. "Temp under the legs is down to three hundred Celsius, Sir. I think we could go outside now."

The Captain nodded gravely.

"Need help with your suit, Bodd?"

"No, child. I have gravity now. That will do."

Twenty minutes later, Icehall leaned against the railing of *J. Edgar Hoover*'s ventral porch and watched his shipmates make their way down the ladder. Boddkluskew in an airsuit was much worse than Boddkluskew in free fall. The tripedal biochemist resembled nothing so much as an overweight methane molecule.

Still, he was far less strange than the welcoming committee: A single man holding a pinlamp stood on the rock outside the blast radius, flanked by fifteen or twenty Rockchompers.

Icehall recalled how he had attempted to describe them to his mother: Start with a bulldog—no, start with a warthog standing on its hind legs, with powerful arms and clawed five-fingered hands. Make it the size of a baby hippopotamus, only with a bigger, longer head. Give it two large, maneuverable eyes protected by bony ridges and three nictitating membranes. For toppers, give it jaws. Square jaws full of huge, chisel-shaped teeth, worked by monstrous muscles that reach back and blend with the massive shoulders. After all, it eats rocks, Mom, really. And there's one more thing…

Icehall listened as Custiss began the introductions.

"Most Esteemed Commander of Castle Harder-Than-The-Midnight-Sky, which employees of the Tripartisan Economic Combine may refer to as Castle Alpha—"

"Did you say, 'Commander?'" interrupted the Captain. "Say, that sounds military. If so, I wasn't briefed on ranks, insignia, or protocol."

"—may I present two distinguished employees of the Tripartisan Economic Combine, who are empowered to initiate trade negotiations, Captain Lionel Bend-Waugh of the starship *Richard M. Nixon*, and Biochemist Boddkluskew-Zhepwulu-Boddkluskew, currently under contract to Pontsalem Adhesives, Inc."

Icehall shook his head and grinned through his teeth. Custiss, the old windbag, had spoken it all in one breath. Then Icehall almost wished to look away, knowing what would come next.

The Commander stuck out his tongue…and shook hands.

Old habit got the Captain through the gesture. Boddkluskew, always mindful of protocol, would have shaken hands with a giant squid. What made Icehall bite his lower lip to keep from laughing was watching the Commander grasp one of the two proffered hands with each side of his large forked tongue, and shake both at once.

It took some getting used to. Each end of the forked tongue was terminated by a boneless, supple four-fingered hand.

Boddkluskew bowed from the waist. "I am most honored, Commander. Would I be out of line in asking your given name?" Boddkluskew was obviously covering for the Captain, who was still staring at his own right hand with a very strange look on his face. Custiss translated the question. The Commander opened his mouth and made a sound like two explosions followed by a scrap crusher on a bad afternoon. Boddkluskew bowed again. "As it is written upon the Nineteen Stones: 'My greenlings will recall the music of your throat down to the seventieth generation.'"

The Commander spoke again, less loudly. Custiss translated as they went. He occasionally asked for clarification by making some alarmingly inhuman noises himself. That had been his job, Icehall reflected, and he had apparently done it well.

"The Commander and I have made arrangements to extend my living quarters to accommodate your party. Your mechanic as well; no need to coop him up in the shuttle."

Right. As though being cooped up in a rock was any better. Icehall began thinking up excuses. Custiss went on.

"Trade negotiations will begin tomorrow, after the welcome feast. The Commander gives both of you his sincerest wishes that your adhesive remain strong under stress."

Icehall chuckled, imagining prudish Captain Bend-Waugh puzzling that one out.

"Uh…Captain, I would recommend bringing the shuttle down on its belly. Earthquakes, you know." Custiss was tapping his foot.

"Yes, yes. Icehall!"

The mechanic gave the Captain a thumbs-up signal and disappeared into the *J. Edgar Hoover*. Icehall watched through a port as the odd party threaded its way back toward the center of the castle. While the ladder slowly eased into its slot and the cargo porch lifted and sealed the port with a wheeze, Icehall thought about Custiss's foot. The man wasn't the twitchy type—but you could pick up a lot of funny habits living alone with unconsolidated aliens for two years.

3.
TURKEY

Icehall poked buttons and rode the shuttle down to horizontal on its lifters. He finished putting things in order before leaving. Then something began hammering hard on the cargo hatch.

Icehall popped the hatch and found himself facing a carbide-grey grin and two wide, saucer-sized eyes.

"Fuller brush man!" the Rockchomper rumbled.

"What?" Icehall could see only poorly into the gloom.

"Don't yank my chain, Amiko! It was in the book! Moses! Yipes! Crippety!"

"Hey! Turkey! Good to see you!" Icehall dropped the hatch's ramp down to the stone pavement so his friend could enter. He thunked the Rockchomper solidly atop the head. "Geez, you're a sight! After riding around with Captain Interruption for six weeks, and no company but Boddkluskew and old Hatchet Face up there … what the heck is a 'fuller brush man?'"

The creature stuck out his tongue with both tongue-hands palm-up, and wiggled his fingertips. Icehall knew that the gesture was the Rockchomper equivalent of a shrug. "Beats my bod. Sheesh. Hobo in the brush biz, verily. Somesuch, mayhap. Wow. Avast."

Icehall shook his head. "Is that how…what's Custiss been teaching you!"

Turkey stomped hard with one heavy foot. The metal of the shuttle rang beneath it. "Nix! Zilch! Diddle! I wouldn't hand him the hose if his hair was on fire! The book! The Book of the Good Words!"

"Oboy." Icehall leaned back on the hull. "You read it."

"Poured it in my ear with a funnel. Yowza. Got it all. Solid, Jackson. Here, test me truly." Turkey reached with half his tongue into a leather pouch hanging around his massive neck. He handed a slender rectangular solid to Icehall, who knew only too well what it was.

He read the title in the multiple moonlight:

A TREASURY OF AMERICAN SLANG AND COLLOQUIALISM
VOLUME 1: 1620-2000

Icehall pushed a button in one corner. "'Fuller brush man,'" he pronounced with exaggerated enunciation.

The book clicked and replied. "'Fuller Brush Man!' A humorous exclamation uttered upon the sudden opening of a door, especially a door upon which one has knocked hard. Used circa 1950-1970. Apparently derived from the sales message of transient brush dealers. See 'Avon Calling.' "

"Goooooooood stuff," Turkey said.

"Oboy. Hey, it was a gag. Really. I mean, people don't talk that way all the time. And some of those terms have been out of date for five hundred years!"

"Forsooth?" The alien looked puzzled.

Icehall shook his head. "You asked me for a dictionary last time before I left. I figured you'd listen to some of the funny words, get a good laugh out of it, and then throw it away."

"Bummer."

"My mother gave it to me for Christmas five years ago. It was supposed to be funny. She always wanted me to be an American teacher, but heck, the voc test said I had 'mechanical aptitude,' and you go where the jobs are. She wrote on the card that if I was going to talk like an illiterate I could at least be good at it."

Turkey's attention was clearly wandering. With one of his tongue-hands he was pinching and poking the material of Icehall's skintights. "How's the weather in there? You air-conditioned, tovarisch?"

Icehall glanced at the lower left corner of his helmet faceplate; the tiny luminous numbers read ten degrees Celsius, with no change detected for the hour they had been grounded. Brisk in a sweater; just right for sweating through a rubber suit. The skintights were not even rated for vacuum. They would keep him comfortable up to perhaps twenty degrees, but that was asking a lot.

"Just as God made me." Icehall fanned an armpit and chuckled. "Does it matter?"

"Yawp! 'Sblood! You're my first Chevy. My proudest possession. My one legal paisan. Heart and my soul's inspiration. Take good care of yourself, you belong to me. When you're hot, you're hot."

"But I'm not. Hey, stop worrying! Custiss said it never gets over twenty here."

Turkey stepped back and clapped his tongue-hands together, a Rockchomper sign of agitation. "Did your mother come from Ireland? Nobody talks about the weather and everybody does something about it. But you. Zip. Ouch."

"I gotta get you a real dictionary," Icehall said, but caught himself looking at the sky.

4.
INTO THE MOUTHLESS ONE

After spending most of the rest of the long Rockchomper night trying to teach Turkey more conventional American, it was all too easy to curl up in the cargo bay with the unlikely creature and fall asleep. Icehall awoke to a hard kick in the side and Custiss standing over him.

"Get this creature out of here! You!" He pointed at Turkey and lapsed into the native language, letting loose a series of throat-ripping grinds. (Get thee hence! 'Twould be my will to have thee feed the smelting ovens!)

Turkey drew back from the advancing man and bowed his head. His reply was soft, and Icehall understood none of it.

(Tempt not thy luck, Star-Burner.)

That done, Turkey leapt out of the hold to the stone below without even touching the ramp, but not before he had squeezed Icehall's shoulder with one tongue-hand. Icehall rose, rubbing his side. He looked out the port after Turkey and watched two other Rockchompers pitching stones at his friend as Turkey fled. Icehall turned to face Custiss.

"I've got ears, Mr. Custiss. You can keep your damned boots to yourself."

Custiss was red-faced furious. "Never let that creature inside this shuttle again. Never ever *ever*! I'll have your job! I'll have your hide! I'll…"

The man must have begun to realize the fool he was making of himself, and leaned back against the bulkhead. He was breathing too quickly, and had the look of a fugitive from death on his face. "Don't mind me. That…Lowest of the Low, I don't trust him. I think he'd like to ruin the shuttle out of spite. He doesn't like us being here. But you won't believe that."

"I don't believe in Santa Claus, either. I think you're stark raving nuts."

Custiss ignored the challenge, pulled a palmstone from his belt and began reading from it. "The Captain would like to have the rest of our supplies brought to our quarters. The Commander sent some porters. Let's get to it."

For an hour Icehall sent crates and machinery down the cargo hatch ramp and helped get it onto the porters' backs. Custiss stood aside and watched, his face grim. The two men led the procession back toward the center of the castle.

Dawn was well underway. Smoky yellow light poured over the crags in the east, between plumes of steam and gas issuing from rents in the mountainsides. The sky was hazy bright, ruddy orange toward the horizons and grey overhead with a tint of green. Castle Alpha was fully lit.

By moonlight the structure was ill-defined and eerie because of its size. By day it was spectacular. The central structure, which Custiss had referred to as the Keep, was an enormous squat stone figure a full hundred meters high. It was the Rockchomper god, which Custiss called The Mouthless One. The body might well have been a fat Rockchomper body resting on its haunches, save that it had fifty or sixty legs spreading outward and downward like tree roots, with busy Rockchompers coming and going between them. The head was wide and flat and had no mouth, only a coiled mothlike proboscis of polished bronze. Five high domed eyes bulged equally spaced around the perimeter of the stone skull. Each was faceted green glass, easily five meters in diameter. Sunlight glittered from the eye that faced east. A row of puckered holes behind the eyes belched grey and black smoke from the metal-working furnaces below.

Four thick stone arms stretched outward and upward from the body. Each bronze-clawed hand gripped what looked very much like a tremendous bronze block and tackle. Turkey would say nothing about them, no matter how much Icehall asked. Cranes?

The rest of the castle was a titanic elliptical mushroom cap three hundred meters across the major axis, and half that across the minor. Small structures dotted the surface here and there, but Icehall knew that most of Rockchomper life went on inside the castle. The main path along the rim of the structure led ultimately between the stone idol's two largest front legs and in through a high, wide portal with hammered copper doors. The shuttle had landed behind the idol's back, near the rearmost extent of the castle, where Custiss had placed the landing beacon.

Along the way around the Keep they passed a construction crew doing repairs on several of the Mouthless One's stone legs. Icehall paused to watch. Perhaps a dozen Rockchompers sat on their squat haunches and shaped stones for the repairs. It was an interesting technique: they held pieces of stone in their front teeth while pounding away with a hammer and chisel held in their tongue-hands.

Somewhere a long way under the surface of Castle Alpha, Icehall's party found a Combine-manufactured steel airlock door glued into the end of a tunnel in the rock. Beyond the airlock door the Captain sat in an easy chair chewn out of red granite and upholstered with a material that Icehall didn't recognize. Boddkluskew puttered among the instruments. A grey box in one corner made electricity for the lights, and another box in the opposite corner was working hard filtering a pungent chemical stink out of the air. An archway with a Combine-built door in it appeared to open into a bathroom. Icehall was glad to get out of his helmet and scratch. If a shower were possible, he was all-in.

"Whatever else you might say about these ugly wogs, Custiss, they do know how to make a good chair."

"Sir, I don't want to stay here tonight," Icehall said as soon as his helmet was on the suit rack by the airlock. Custiss gave him a poisonous look.

The Captain shook his head. "Oh, bosh. Wait until you see the beds they've made for us. Three meters square and soft as goose down—a man could get lost in one."

"I prefer small, hard beds. What's this funny stuff all over the walls for?" Icehall ran a hand across the wall next to the airlock. It was coated with a pale green foamy material, like frozen froth from a lime phosphate. He pushed and it gave a little. He pushed harder and felt solid rock a decimeter beneath.

"Insulation, and a vapor barrier," Custiss said. "I found that after awhile the bare stone walls made moisture condense out of the air. Made things clammy and damp. After all, this was my home for two years."

"They use a similar foam for the chair cushions, and an even softer foam for the beds," said the Captain. "I wonder how they make it."

Icehall knew how, and hoped the Captain never found out. "I think it makes the place feel like a padded cell. Look, Sir, Mr. Custiss has been hammering on how worried he is about the safety of the shuttle from earthquakes. If it's really that bad, I think I ought to take the shuttle back up to the ship until we're ready to leave. With all this padding you're probably quite safe from banging around in here, and I'll be about as useful as a third le…um, do you get my point, Sir?"

The Captain started nodding. "You know, that might be worth it after all. I think…"

"Out of the question!" Custiss exploded. "The Commander would be gravely offended!"

Icehall made a face. "Oh, come *on*, Mr. Custiss!"

The Captain paled. "No...wouldn't want that, no, not at all. Look, let's argue about this later on, say, men? I'm sure we all have better things to do. You too, Mr. Icehall. Make sure your dress blues are pressed. I won't have you looking the grease monkey for the feast tomorrow."

Icehall got away as soon as he could. He had never been at ease around Custiss, and now could barely stand to be in the same room with the man. Icehall had not gone forty steps down the stone corridor before Turkey dropped out of a tunnel worming away through a hole in the low ceiling. "Hail and farewell! Hubba-hubba!" the creature said, and fell into step alongside him.

"Custiss is going to drive me crazy," Icehall complained.

"Heesh! You and me brother. Hey, let's blow this pop stand and see some sights!" Turkey, as was his way, took off at a slow gallop on all fours. Icehall sighed and trotted along after him.

Icehall thought he saw why his friend preferred to move quickly. Everywhere Turkey went, other Rockchompers would throw things at him and poke at him with sticks and tools. Furthermore, Icehall got the impression that the populace was generally on good behavior when citizens of the Combine were about—he hated to imagine how his friend was treated in the crew's absence.

Every so often, Turkey would pause and do a sort of tap-dance on his hind legs while the pebbles and trash pelted him. Icehall ducked out of the way as much as he could until the display was over.

"My public," Turkey said in his rumbly voice, but would not otherwise explain.

They left the Keep at a trot and immediately made for a point on the castle's perimeter. A spiral ramp began there and wound for two and a half turns around the entire structure before the castle merged with a jumble of lava slabs and hillocks of igneous rock on the valley floor.

Turkey started down the ramp at his usual rapid pace. Icehall had to call him back many times. The ramp was never wider than two meters, at times narrowing to one, and the Rockchompers had not yet invented railings. Icehall got an uncomfortably vivid aerial view of the surrounding valley and some of the other castles.

A dozen or so roads radiated away from the castle, splitting and bending and forking until Icehall lost sight of them in the volcanic haze. He could make out groups of Rockchompers working near the roads, and a regular ribbing pattern here and there that indicated cultivation.

Several times they had to stop and squeeze back against the castle wall to let lines of laborers pass, each carrying a hod of broken stone or grotesque vegetables on his back. Close to the bottom, a herdsman was beating a waddling crew of animals up the ramp toward the castle. The beasts were caricatures of dachshunds, but scaled, and each had a membranous model of a suspension bridge on its back.

Icehall had always thought it odd that the castles of Castle Valley grew narrow toward their bases. When he and Turkey finally leapt from the ramp down onto the rocky valley floor, he saw with some surprise that a crew of at least a hundred Rockchompers were at work pounding, chiseling, and gnawing rock away from the base of the castle, further undermining its already questionable foundations. The walls of the structure swelled outward and hung above them.

"Why are they doing that?" Icehall asked.

"Couldn't tell you," Turkey said too quickly, and Icehall wondered how he meant it.

5.

FROM THE "TELL ME MORE, MR. WIZARD!" LIBRARY

Icehall followed Turkey down a paved road, then over a rocky path between rows of nondescript yellow-green plants, each bearing a crown of slimy-looking brown fronds. The path forked and narrowed and finally vanished amid heaps of volcanic slag and stands of brittle-looking weeds.

Turkey pressed on at a lumbering trot, leaping over meter-wide crevasses that Icehall had to pause and consider. Each time he swore he would not leap another, and each time he held his breath and kicked off. Eventually the worst happened: Up ahead, Turkey came upon on a gaping crack in the rock, and dropped out of sight. Icehall yelled and galloped up to the hole. Cautiously he peered over the edge—

"Boogah!" the Rockchomper bellowed, then broke into gales of laughter. Turkey was standing in a low lava cave where the roof had collapsed. Without apologizing for the fright or pausing to explain, Turkey turned and plodded off into the cave. Icehall dropped over the edge himself, grit his teeth, pulled out his belt lamp, and followed.

The cave wound like the intestine of a snake, black and scaled with conchoidal facets of fractured obsidian. Now and then, around a curve, there would be light from another rent in the ceiling, and Icehall would see his friend far ahead, trotting heedlessly onward on all fours.

Arches in agony, Icehall finally emerged blinking into daylight. The place was a vast hollow, a lava cavern without a roof but with glassy, striated walls, towering and unscalable. It had probably been a titanic gas bubble that had burst upward and outward while the rock around it had not yet hardened;

near the tops of the walls were weird lava projections and formations like gray-black teeth.

Turkey was at the opposite wall, sitting in a very large stone chair obviously chewed out of solid rock. All around him were piles of stones, tools, bits of metal, wire, and glass.

"Makes the blood flow, eh wot?"

Icehall shook his head and grinned. "You had better have an *awful* good reason for putting me through this."

"A-Number-One. Nothing but the best." Turkey waved his tongue-hands in every direction. "Yahsure, my Sanctum Sanctorum. My hidey-hole. Nobody here but us Turkeys."

Icehall began to understand. "Ahhhhhh. Getting away from the madding crowds, huh? Weird kind of place, but it suits."

"Got to do my own thing now and then. Dig? I dig."

Turkey left his chair and made a motion to follow with one of his tongue-hands. He vanished through a short tunnel and into another, much larger lava cave. Icehall reluctantly followed.

It was not a long trip. A hundred meters in Icehall felt a tongue-hand wrap around his forearm. He peered into the gloom and saw that the floor abruptly ended two meters ahead.

Icehall's eyes grew used to the darkness. All along the obsidian-bejeweled walls and crowding up to the edge of this new chasm were vine-like plants with glistening glassy trunks as thick as his forearm. Icehall shone his light on one and saw within the transparent stalk a vein with brownish fluid coursing through it in slow, pumping contractions. Beside it another vein carried the same fluid in the opposite direction. Toward its crown, the plant branched into many smaller stalks, each terminating in a cluster of rectangular brown fruits looking like nothing more than ten-kilo chocolate bars. Turkey, seeing his interest, snatched one from its branch and handed it to Icehall.

Icehall yelped and dropped it; the thing was *hot*.

"Yeep! Sorry about that, Chief." Turkey picked the fruit from the floor and bit it in half. Steaming brown gook oozed from the severed ends. "You have to develop a taste for it."

"No thanks," Icehall said. He got down on hands and knees and crept to the edge of the vast emptiness. The feeble beam from his helmet lamp was lost before it descended a hundred meters. Wraiths of vapor drifted about the cavern, and the draft creeping over him was uncomfortably warm. Then, on a hunch, Icehall extinguished his lamp.

After a few seconds he saw that the depths were illuminated by a weak orange glow. Icehall saw the glassy trunks twisting their way down the sheer rock face toward whatever geological inferno lay below. It made sense in a moment: Heat exchangers on each end, and a pump every half meter along the way between.

"Hot stuff down there," Turkey muttered.

"I guess." Icehall crept back from the edge and got to his feet. "Is this some kind of warning?"

Turkey was already pulling him to one side of the passage. "Nope. Job application."

There was a pedestal chewed out of a lava stalagmite, and atop the pedestal was…something. A heavy iron wagon wheel rested horizontally on crude bearings, within a cage supporting six solenoids, each wound from wire as thick as a soda straw. It was at once alien and terribly familiar, reminding him of the oversimplified diagrams of electric motors to be found in grade school science books.

Almost hidden by the stone pedestal was a smaller pillar on which rested a caricature of an old-fashioned incandescent light bulb, crudely blown from grainy blue-green glass, including the little curl at the top.

"Win a few, lose a few," Turkey said a little sadly, and with one tongue-hand grasped the iron wheel at its edge and gave the wheel a hard spin. It creaked to an unsteady halt after fifteen or twenty turns.

"Good grief! A dynamo!" Icehall pulled a wrench from his belt and felt magnetism draw it toward the black iron wheel. He traced the fat copper wires from solenoid to solenoid and down to the lumpy glass bulb. The bulb lifted in his hands— and the wires stayed behind. The glass envelope was not sealed, much less evacuated, and was simply resting over the three curls of millimeter-thick wire that Icehall imagined to be the filament.

That seemed suspicious. "What sort of plan were you building from?"

Turkey hung his head for a moment, then galloped off. He returned shortly with another book in his hand. Icehall read the title with his belt-lamp:

ELECTRICITY CAN BE YOUR FRIEND!

A "TELL ME MORE, MR. WIZARD!" BOOK

Turkey pressed a button on the book's side. "Tell me more about generators, Mr. Wizard!" he commanded.

The back cover of the book abruptly lit up with a colorful animation of a dynamo very much like Turkey's model. The wheel began to turn, and little green balls with legs and tiny smiling faces began dashing along the conductors. The book spoke in a rapid, nasal, somewhat breathless man's voice. "Sure, Turkey! When the magnetic wheel turns, magnetic lines of force make whole armies of tiny little electrons march along the copper wires. But when they all try to rush through the much tinier wires in the lamp bulb, they bump against one another! And do you know what happens then?"

"No, tell me what happens then, Mr. Wizard!" Turkey asked, in a voice that matched the book's voice in both enthusiasm and breathlessness.

"They bump together so much that they get hot and the wire starts emitting light!"

Icehall snatched the book from Turkey's grip and thumbed it off. "Where did you get that?"

Turkey hung his head. "I cannot tell a lie. I ripped it off."

"You what?"

"Snatched it. Swiped it. Five-finger discount. Spirited it away. Copped it. Shoplifted it. See 'fell of the back of a truck.'"

"From Custiss?"

Turkey nodded slowly.

Icehall lost control. He roared, falling against the stone wall and curling up in a fetal position on the floor. Turkey cocked his head to one side, puzzled. "Giggles?"

It was some time before Icehall could speak coherently again. "So much for the virtues of a liberal education. I'll bet he has the whole 'Tell Me More, Mr. Wizard!' library." Icehall reached between the hammered-iron members of the dynamo's cage and spun the lodestone wheel again. "You did a pretty fine job, considering the source of your blueprints. Just for fun?"

"Nay, nay! It's my final exam, my union card, my master's thesis!"

"Before you said something about a job application, but what with that dictionary…"

"Scope me, chuck! I'm a workin' man! And this burg's done worked out."

"So…you want to go back with us…and work for the Combine?"

"Throw the gentleman a fish!"

Icehall began to nod. "And you built this to prove to us you were worth something. I…I'm impressed."

"Hic! Hogsnort. Blather. I left it hangin'. Had a master plan: Dip the hot vegetables in a pot, cover and simmer, blow steam on a fan, turn the wheel, light the lamp, shine the light, everything's gonna be allright! But I blew it." Turkey spun the wheel again and looked dolefully at the three little curls of wire forming the "bulb"'s filament. "More heat than light. Alack! No heat either."

"Hold on a sec. Just hold on. Helmet! Rough cut: How many amperes would it take to make a short length of 2 millimeter diameter copper wire emit visible light?"

Icehall's helmet replied immediately. "Rough cut: Two hundred twenty amperes. Precise calculations will depend on wavelength of emitted light, ambient temperature, purity of copper, and exact length of wire."

Two hundred twenty amps! Rough cut or not, that was a lot of current, even for a genuine dynamo. Icehall pulled the field analyzer from his belt kit and set it for current measurement. He held it close to the copper filament that wouldn't glow. "Spin the wheel." Turkey again gave the rotor a push and closed his huge eyes, wincing.

"Six point six amperes, average," peeped the analyzer.

Icehall felt a rush of wonder. Turkey had scratch-built a working electric generator from a cartoon out of a book written for eight-year-olds. "You're hired."

6.

WELCOME FEAST

Icehall always felt like a fool, eating in dress uniform in an alien atmosphere. The Exogourmet Mark III helmet was a bulbous transparent plastic box starting behind his head and extending down over his chest almost to his waist. On each side of the box was a hole leading into a plastic glove, so that a wearer could insert his hands and feed himself. Internal pressure regulation was poor; if you sneezed too hard you ended up with two extra plastic hands flapping from the sides of your helmet.

Evidently Icehall was alone in disliking the Exogourmet; the others were enjoying themselves. Custiss reached into a box beside his stone chair and passed out sealed cylinders containing the main course, chicken Kiev. Icehall looked down and wrinkled his nose at the picked-over remains of the previous course. Avocado quiche had never been a favorite of his, either. He twisted its cylinder and yanked hard until it came loose, then shoved the new cylinder home and turned it around until the seal broke and the chicken rotated into view. Overdone and too much garlic, he thought. This would not be a feast to remember.

To the right of the Captain, the Commander was popping pebbles into the air with one tongue-hand, and catching them and tossing them down his cavernous throat with the other. In another corner of the room five Rockchompers were doing what Icehall imagined was music. It consisted of hammering madly at an amorphous collection of stone chimes and drums. All around the hall Rockchompers were sitting on their stocky haunches, wolfing down copper trays and bowls of pebbles, stringy grey vegetables, gruesome platters of raw, orange-tinted meat, and what looked a lot like ready-mix concrete.

"Excellent feast, excellent," the Captain said to the Commander, who grated his pleasure after Custiss translated.

"Really, Captain, I believe I can almost pick out a tonal pattern in our entertainment. They're actually quite good, I think." Boddkluskew masticated a large chunk of chicken. "Though my tastes are often questionable."

"Makes me want to get up, get out and dance," Icehall muttered, "but mostly it just makes me want to get up and get out."

The Commander picked up a large stone mallet shaped like a huge clawed leg chewed off at the hip, and swung it at a copper gong suspended beside his throne. Several Rockchompers trotted into the throne room on their hind legs, almost on tiptoe. They made a complicated series of tongue-hand signals to each other and to the throne, and then without warning began throwing rocks at one another.

Icehall watched, apprehensive. The jesters played with vigor; if one of those rocks came his way he was ducking under the table, and to hell with dignity. The ragged *thwok!* of stone against Rockchomper hide was painful to hear. The throng in the audience seemed to think it was great fun.

The Commander rang the gong again. Moments later, Icehall leapt to his feet after spraying chicken Kiev all over the inside of his helmet.

A crew of six Rockchomper porters was carrying Turkey into the room, upside-down on a huge bronze platter.

The crowd was roaring with what Icehall recognized as laughter and approval. Turkey was lying on a bed of slimy gray-green Rockchomper garnish. His legs were tied together, and dribbles of viscous green sauce oozed down along his sides. Behind the procession marched an old, bent-backed Rockchomper carrying the biggest saw Icehall had ever seen.

Custiss was roaring with laughter. The Commander was bellowing to the crowd, who were bellowing in return and making elaborate signs with their tongue-hands.

"Custiss, what's going on!" Icehall hissed.

Custiss giggled. "They're deciding whether or not to eat the Lowest of the Low."

"Damn! I vote no!" Icehall yelled.

"Sit down and shut up. Nobody asked you."

"Captain, I object!"

"Come come, be a sport, Icehall," the Captain said, a queasy note in his voice. "This is supposed to be *fun*."

Icehall kept quiet after that. He was fairly certain that the Rockchompers were not cannibals, but...they *were* unconsolidated aliens, after all. Turkey rolled an eyeball his way and wiggled several of the clawed fingers on his front legs. The old Rockchomper, whom Icehall now recognized as the Commander's personal cook, hobbled around the bronze platter, poking Turkey here and there with a large fork and making comments that the crowd evidently found hilarious. Twice he poured stone urns of sauce over the upended creature, and several times he whacked the butt of the saw against Turkey's massive jawbone.

The cook turned and gestured to the Commander. The Commander stood, made some slightly subdued grating noises that suggested hesitation, and then waved his tongue-hands rapidly back and forth. The crowd let go a gravelly groan of disappointment.

"The Commander says he can't allow the serving of spoiled meat in front of his distinguished guests from the stars. Maybe next time. Shame," Custiss said.

The Commander turned to the Captain and asked a question. Custiss was quick to translate.

"He asked me if your 'lowest of the low' knows any tricks to entertain us with."

The Captain looked at Icehall. Icehall grimaced. "I know how to disappear in an awful hurry." Icehall started to rise. The Captain laid a hand on his shoulder and shoved him back into his seat.

The old cook sawed the ropes away from Turkey's legs. Turkey wriggled his fingers and toes and rolled off the platter, dropping sticky garnish on the floor. Someone tossed a fist-sized rock at him. Turkey caught it in his teeth, saw two more coming, and caught them in his clawed front hands. He spat the first stone into the air, tossed the other two after it, and started to juggle them. Half a dozen more rocks came his way. He swallowed several and added the rest to the string of stones flying in a neat arc from one hand to the other. Icehall stood up and applauded. Turkey rolled his eyes, rocked back on his tail, opened his mouth, and began to juggle three more stones with his tongue-hands, this time in the opposite direction.

"Truly, he should go into politics!" Boddkluskew observed.

The Rockchomper crowd did not agree. From across the room one of them stood and threw a stone plate as large as a saucer sled. It hit Turkey on the back of the head and shattered. Shards flew in all directions. In moments the air was full of food, plates, urns and mugs, smashing on the floor or thunking against Turkey's rugged hide. Turkey let his juggling stones drop down his throat, then lowered his head and beat a hasty retreat through a low, wide tunnel to one side. Icehall waited until the shower of crockery had ceased, then slipped past Boddkluskew and followed.

In a dank corner of the castle's cavernous kitchen, Icehall heaved buckets of water over his friend to dilute the sticky sauce, and picked bits of garnish from the chinks between the fibrous scales covering his skin. "I don't know why you put up with that kind of nonsense."

"No sweat. Whillickers. It's my *yob*, mon."

"Well, then I think it's high time you got promoted."

Icehall knew he had a lot to learn about Rockchomper facial expression, but he could tell the idea disturbed Turkey.

"Hoo boy! Goodness gracious. Pshaw! True dat. Que sera, sera. Let's whistle past the graveyard. Tell me body true: Is this trip really necessary?"

Icehall was puzzled. "Boddkluskew's company expects to make some money from it. All they want to do is arrange for your people to…er…make some glue into cans so they can sell it. In return they'll be trading tools, metal, chemicals, things like that. Benefits on both sides. That's how we do things up there." Icehall raised his eyes ceilingward.

"Not just tonight but for always?"

Another peculiar question. "Economic systems evolve. Eventually you'll have your own starships and your own emergent industry. It'll take a while. Years, maybe…"

Turkey looked down at the ground. He seemed to be thinking hard. "Arrgh. Marry! That's a tall order. Heesh! Why me, Lord? See here, Watson. Turn some screws. Grease some wheels. Do yourself a favor. Get off the planet…pronto! Make like a tree and leave! Come back when the heat's off! Ulp…"

Turkey's front legs buckled, and the creature pitched forward on his face. His triple nictitating membranes winked into place and the leathery folds of his eyelids pressed shut, as though he were in pain.

"Hey, what's wrong?" Icehall suppressed a shiver and got down on his knees.

Turkey's eyes opened halfway. "Indigestion?"

Icehall grimaced, then swore. "I don't believe that. You want to get out of here too, well, I'll do what I can, but you have to be square with me. You're sitting on something. If we're in danger we can leave any time, but we have to know what the danger is. What do you think will happen when I go to the Captain and insist we leave in the middle of a big trade powwow because the village idiot thinks it'd be better that way? Custiss could get the Captain to order me to quarters and not talk to you anymore. You want that? What's going on? Tell me!"

Turkey pushed his knees together and got to his feet again. "Mmmph. The truth hurts. Ouch. Forgive us our trespasses. Eek! Must close for now. Gotta go downtown and bum around. Meet me in St. Louis."

"What?"

"Spot me hanging around the main gate. 1100 shiptime."

"Since when can you tell shiptime?"

Turkey rummaged in his neck pouch, and when his tongue-hands emerged, one was wearing a shiny digital watch. "Sticky fingers and loose morals," the creature explained. "Go west, young man! A thousand pardons! Criminy!" Turkey took off through another dim passageway at a run. Only then did Icehall notice his helmet beeping at him. The Captain wanted him back at the dinner table.

7.

THE BLACK WIDOW
WORKER AUTORETRIEVAL DEVICE

At the Captain's orders, Icehall had changed into a heavy-duty Rabinowicz armored pressure suit, and was now standing impatiently in the middle of the dining hall, listening to Boddkluskew lecture. Icehall detested being used as a fashion model, but he did enjoy wearing the Rabinowicz. It was more expensive by an order of magnitude than any suit he had ever been issued. The model he was wearing was rated from seventy-five degrees Kelvin on the bootsoles to seven hundred degrees Kelvin at half an atmosphere continuous, with the rating extended in both directions for limited periods of time. The faceplate was a twelve-layer tunable image translator, capable of displaying incoming radiation from long infrared to low gammas as visible light. The suit was widely used by heavy metal mining companies excavating on fire-zone planets.

Boddkluskew had just finished his long-winded explanation of what Pontsalem Adhesives needed quick-setting glues for. Now, Icehall thought, for the demonstration.

"… so we can show you how it works. The Pontsalem Black Widow Worker Autoretrieval Device has been attached to the suit Icehall is wearing. Carefully watch the black cowling covering the right forearm of the suit. Icehall, please demonstrate."

Custiss finished translating the last few sentences. Icehall leapt up atop a long, tall stone table that a pair of Rockchompers had moved to the center of the dining hall. The Rabinowicz's hydraulic knees made it much easier than it might otherwise have been.

Icehall sighed and took two running steps down the length of the table, and leapt off the edge. He pointed his right arm at the ceiling and made a very tight fist. A bone-grinding concussion shook the length of his arm. A pencil-sized projectile left one of the three holes in the wrist end of the black cowling with a sharp whine, trailing a cord. The projectile struck the ceiling with a loud report and stayed there. A moment later Icehall, still a meter above the floor, hit the end of his rope.

The cord ripped free of the black cowling, ripped away from tethers down the length of the suit's right arm, and reached its mounting point on a harness over Icehall's navel. Icehall grunted and regained his breath. He pressed a button on the wrist cowling and a winch inside the harness began taking up line. Swinging like a plumb bob, Icehall approached the stone ceiling.

Boddkluskew went on. "A worker engaged in exploring hazardous surroundings need not fear death by falling from precipitous heights. He need merely direct his hand toward a nearby point of support, and he can be suspended safely while calling for assistance via suit radio. There is only one drawback to the device."

Icehall cringed. He had heard little else from Boddkluskew during the long trip to Scattershot.

Boddklusku went on, eyes down. "One out of three adhesive capsules fails to set quickly enough to support a worker's weight. We have provided three projectiles in each cowling, but there is some question as to whether a worker falling to his death would have the presence of mind to rapidly fire them at a suitable point of support. And, of course, there is that plaguey one-in-twenty-seven chance that all three capsules will fail. This bodes poorly for the survival of the worker. Quite honestly, this defect is beginning to hurt our quarterly sales growth curves. We at Pontsalem Adhesives have an ongoing need for a substance that can be made to set within one hundred milliseconds and support a thousand kilos per square centimeter randomly distributed upon impact. We would like the opportunity to sample and test your...*adhesive* for suitability."

Custiss finished translating. *His throat must lift weights,* Icehall thought, still hanging from the ceiling.

The Commander rose from his throne. He drew an iron weapon from a rack above his head. It was an ugly serrated sword, more than two meters long, looking like nothing more than a gigantic frozen-food knife. The Commander casually bit off most of the length of the blade, leaving a blunt, thick stub set into the massive hilt.

The Commander strolled to the center of the dining hall, squatted, lifted his tail, and defecated a mass of pale yellow ooze on the floor. The Captain's eyes widened.

"I don't believe what he just did! Custiss, have we offended him? Boddkluskew, this is disgraceful!"

"Business is business, Captain, on Earth or anywhere else. Please bear with us," Custiss said.

The Commander turned and dipped the stub of the weapon in the gobbet of ooze and spread it about on the blade. He inspected the end with a critical eye for a moment, then turned and spat a wad of green ichor high on the closest wall. The Captain was holding his head in his hands. Icehall felt sorry for him; Bend-Waugh was hardly the right man for this job.

The Commander hefted the truncated weapon in one of his clawed front hands. With a grinding shout he ran for the wall on his hind legs and leapt at the small spot of spittle. He slammed the edge of the blade into the green spot and hung there, five hundred kilos massive, bellowing to the crowd and waving his tongue-hands in the air. At the Commander's signal one of his guards left his place by the throne and climbed the Commander's tail until there were two Rockchompers hanging three meters off the floor on one small spot of "glue."

"Gentlemen, let us bargain," Boddkluskew said slowly and with obvious amazement.

That evening, Icehall listened while Custiss attempted to explain Rockchomper biology to squeamish Captain Bend-Waugh.

"They've undergone considerable post-mammalian evolution, Sir. It's marvelous! They passed through a conventional mammalian stage eons ago, but rather than developing a massive cortex immediately as we did, theirs evolved slowly over millions of years, and evolved along with a body chemistry unlike anything we've seen before.

"Humans ingest food, use food energy for life processes and protein to build body structures, and produce toxic wastes in the process which must be separated from the body to prevent damage. Compared to Rockchomper chemistry, ours is simple and terribly crude. They can ingest almost any-thing—rock, metal, vegetation, meat animals—and they use everything. What isn't used for respiration and cell production becomes raw material for the miniature chemical factory along their digestive tracts. What you assumed was excrement was actually a plastic that can be made to set quickly—as we saw—or more slowly. It can be made transparent or opaque, and it can be resoftened and reworked at any time. It can be made to harden so quickly that it catches fire; they never needed flint and steel.

"At will, they can create a solvent for dissolving any given type of rock quickly and cleanly. Tunnels here aren't dug; they're chemically bored right through solid rock. They don't waste anything that they eat. Whatever inert substances they ingest are used as filler for their 'adhesive.' This whole structure was assembled stone by stone and glued together without a single steel reinforcing beam, yet it is strong enough to withstand—"

"To withstand *what*, Mr. Custiss?" Icehall asked sharply.

Custiss chewed his lip for a moment. "Earthquakes. You may have noticed how Castle Alpha narrows toward the base. Actually, it is not attached to the ground at all, but merely rests upon it, so that if the ground shifts, Castle Alpha shifts with it and remains perfectly horizontal at all times, without damage. There are serious earthquakes here, Mr. Icehall. There was a respectable temblor last night, if I recall."

"I must have slept through it," the Captain said.

Icehall, by contrast, slept very little after the crew of the *Nixon* turned in that night. Castle Alpha was a marvelous place, peopled by marvelous beings. The more he saw of the Commander, the more he saw of the crisp discipline with which the Commander led his people, the more the whole arrangement began to look familiar. On the edge of a fitful dream he realized what Castle Alpha reminded him of:

It reminded him of a battleship.

8.

FIREJAMMER

Icehall's wrist alarm began feeping at 1045. Before leaving his sleeping nook, he pulled on his skintights and clamped their life support ring around his waist. With his helmet tucked underneath his arm he looked in on his crewmates. The Captain was sleeping like a baby with the covers pulled over his head. Boddkluskew was wheezing rhythmically through his slitlike nostrils, sleeping upright on all threes (as his kind always slept) with knees locked. In front of the old Phelgre his palmstone was patiently reminding him that it was his move and he was in check. With growing alarm Icehall realized that Custiss was nowhere in their custom-built padded cell, and his space-rated pressure suit was no longer on the rack.

Icehall cycled the airlock and padded toward the main surface entrance. Everywhere around him Rockchompers were hauling crates on carts and rushing about through the wide, low hallways lit by flickering torches. Twice he stopped, and leaned against the passage wall while it shifted one way from vertical and then the next. Temblor! The Rockchompers didn't even break stride when the land beneath Castle Alpha shifted. Icehall borrowed some courage from their nonchalance and walked on.

The shadows among the stone legs of the Mouthless One were many and deep. Icehall kept to them, squinting into the gloom cast by scattered torches and several moons overhead. The thirty-seven hour Scattershot day was playing hob with his biological clock; his stomach would be expecting breakfast soon, and here night had only just fallen. Another small temblor rumbled Castle Alpha's foundations. Icehall leaned against a stone leg and tried to quiet his heart's hammering. A pebble went *snap!* against the polymer of his helmet, and when he whirled about in a panic he saw Turkey sitting on his haunches in deeper shadow.

"The walls have ears. The night has a thousand eyes. Uneasy rests the head that wears the crown. Something is rotten in the state of Denmark ..."

"All right, already! I get the idea. *Be* coy if you want. Look, Custiss snuck out on us last night, and he took a suit that'll see him through a lot. He must have been watching me, because I spent most of last night watching *him*. I've got to get to the shuttle, to see what's up. Blast it all, will you tell me what's going on?"

"Urrrp-shhhh!" Turkey put a tongue-hand on each of Icehall's shoulders and shoved him to the ground. Out of the main entrance to the Keep marched a file of very large Rockchompers, each carrying a serrated weapon like the one the Commander had bitten in two during the Black Widow demonstration. Icehall counted forty-four of them.

"Commander's hotshot guard. Badass dudes, every mother's son. Shucks! Eek! Button your lip and follow the leader!"

Turkey turned and padded deeper into the forest of stone columns that supported the Keep. Icehall followed as quickly as he could, arms outstretched to keep him from braining himself in the dark. They worked their way one hundred eighty degrees around the Keep, to where they could see the Commander's guard take up formation, nose to tail, around the *J. Edgar Hoover*.

"Oboy," whispered Icehall.

"Bare bones o' God! Ain't we got fun! Nertz! Excelsior!"

Icehall followed Turkey further around to the western side of the Keep, where, with fewer moons in the west, the darkness was nearly total. The pair dashed between outbuildings, keeping to shadows, and finally stopped at the very edge of Castle Alpha. There was no railing. Icehall fought back acrophobia and clamped both hands onto the end of Turkey's tail. Tail in hand, Icehall crept up toward the dropoff.

The view was southwestward, down the length of Castle Valley. Icehall could count a full dozen other castles in the distance. All of them seemed ablaze with bonfires and activity. Across the valley floor he could make out tiny flickering torchlight processions creeping their way toward one castle or another, each light a faint yellow star on the edge of visibility. Looking down, Icehall counted fifteen or twenty such torchlight parades converging on Castle Alpha. But where were the Commander's bonfires? The upper surface of the Castle was hung with impenetrable night, and virtually devoid of life.

Turkey pointed to the columns of light creeping toward the base of Castle Alpha. "Chickens coming home to roost. Jeepers creepers! This is the day the Lord has made."

"You're making less sense the longer I listen to you. Talk to me, for—"

The rock around them shook, harder this time than ever before. Turkey hunkered down and dug his claws into the cracks in the stone. Icehall dropped his grip on Turkey's tail and wrapped both arms around Turkey's massive left leg. The subsonic rumble made the sweat stand out on his forehead and drip toward his eyes. When the quake subsided, Icehall gave the scaly haunch a hard whack with his fist.

"If you don't explain right now I'm leaving. I'm going back to my little hole in the rock and play Masters of Mayhem until the mission is over, and I'll be damned if I'll ever say another word to you again."

Turkey lowered his head until the tip of his nose touched the rock. He kept that position for several silent minutes while only the constant puffing and relaxing of his sides indicated that he was alive. Icehall felt a shivering begin in the stone-hard flanks that did not subside. Turkey groaned, and turned to look at him with half-lidded eyes.

"Way down in the valley, the valley so low—mercy!—I opened your eyes to a crack. Right in the middle, up and back, from Christopher to madness, where there be valley there be crack, by gully! Down, down, down she goes, where she stops, cripes! Hellfire and then some. Custiss had a word…*tectonic discontinuity*, by jingo! We-uns is mugwumps; mugs on one side of the fence, wumps on t'other. Custiss read our natural history to us, with commentary, Mr. And Mrs. America! Sixteen moons, grade triple-A jumbo, king-size plus tax, all line up just so every two hundred four years. A situation of much gravity. Ulp! Tears hell out of the crust, makes for a parting of plates. Magma rises—fills the valley. Ouch! Bloody! We're ships that pass in the night! Zounds! Do you hear me, little brother?" The shivering in Turkey's body intensified. The creature seemed to be enduring intense pain.

"I hear you. Wow. The valley turns into a sea of molten rock, and each castle becomes a ship. It must be a battle just to survive such a thing."

Turkey thumped the ground with his tail. "Battle! Nuts! We have not yet begun to fight. Blood, tears, toil, and sweat! War is hell! You ain't seen nuthin' yet! Behold…out thataway, by the light of the silvery moon, a hillock, round and smooth." Turkey's hand indicated a foothill a few kilometers down the valley. "That was a castle that didn't make it, last time around. Split wide open! Busted! Bought the farm! Turned over…sank."

Icehall was horrified. "You sound as though you were there."

Turkey's voice grew soft. "I saw it with mine own eyes. The Commander was at the helm…gave the order to ram. On our hands! Ugh. Yekkh!"

Icehall felt a shiver run down his own spine. "Battleships, on an ocean of molten rock. This is too much! That means that all those pulleys and ropes up there in the Mouthless One's hands are for furling and steering sails? A fleet of warring firejammers…why didn't you tell us!"

Turkey's eyes closed. For a moment he seemed to be whimpering to himself. "I have sworn a deadly oath. Cross my heart and hope to die. It's in the blood! Dratz! I am a prisoner of the heart—my heart—endless agony the price if I betray my…my…"

"Your what?"

"Commander!" Turkey spat. "'Tis a tale told by an idiot. Goldurn! But you haven't heard the half of it. Check it out!"

Turkey turned, and Icehall turned with him. Two more moons had joined their fellows in the eastern sky, and the light was better now. Icehall sucked in his breath, then muttered an angry curse.

The Rockchomper guard had lined up on either side of shuttle *J. Edgar Hoover*, and were now carrying it slowly toward the rearmost point of Castle Alpha.

"They're going to throw it overboard! I'll kill! Kill!"

"Peace, brother." Turkey laid a tongue-hand on each of Icehall's shoulders and gently pressed him back down into a crouch. Icehall forced himself to think clearly. He knew to the kilogram what the *J. Edgar Hoover* weighed, and mentally calculated the load split forty-four ways. Still considerable. The Rockchompers were hellishly strong.

Icehall watched the rest of the procession in silence. The Rockchomper guard carried the shuttle rearward until the flared end of the fusion tube projected a meter over the edge of the rock. There they set the spacecraft down, turned nose-for-tail, and began defecating on it.

Icehall's jaw dropped abruptly as the whole scheme became clear. Sails were suddenly passé in *this* war. Scattershot's first fusion-powered firejammer was under construction.

"Turkey, we gotta go warn the Captain. Or do *something*."

Turkey shook his head. "Yippers. Easier said than done. Nertz! Follow me, Bwana."

9.

"Guard Thy Belly, Bastard!"

Icehall assumed that there would be an all-points bulletin out for himself and Turkey by that time, but none of the Rockchompers they encountered challenged them. Three more temblors of increasing violence made Icehall fall on his face as they wormed their way down toward the *Nixon's* crew's quarters. When Turkey and Icehall drew up on the air-lock door, they found a smooth bead of Rockchomper adhesive around the door seam, and a very large guard with an ugly serrated weapon.

Turkey and the guard immediately growled and grated at one another.

(Lowest of the Low! The Commander hast given the order that thou must go unto him and serve him. Why hast this Star-Burner not been sealed in with his fellows?)

(The Star-Burner is my prisoner. I will bear him unto the Commander when I obey the order. Mouthless One carry you through this Day of Fire! I go!)

"Turkey! What's happening!"

"Time is tight. Too much talk and not enough action! Damn the torpedoes! Let's split!"

Once more Turkey trotted down the hall, Icehall stumbling behind. The temblors had become fairly constant, and only the worst of them made Icehall stop. They found their way to a central shaft with a spiral stair cut like the thread of a screw into the rock wall. It was plainly inside the very center of the Keep. Turkey started up the stair at a run. Icehall hesitated. There was no railing, and the shaft seemed to go down a *long* way. He heard Turkey whistling high above.

Icehall steeled himself and followed, leaning on the inner wall and gripping what crannies he could find.

Up they climbed, through the center of the Keep, up through the body of the Mouthless One. A particularly violent temblor nearly threw Icehall over the edge of the stairway. It was many minutes before he would move again.

At the top of the stair was a ring of torches, burning bright amidst curls of acrid, heavy smoke, and three guards arranged before an enormous vaulted copper door. Hammered into the door was an image of a castle riding high on a sea of writhing flames. The guards incongruously stood aside without a word and allowed Turkey to push the door inward.

They were inside the Mouthless One's head. At the center of the room was a bronze throne, the real ruling throne, trimmed with iron and silver. The throne stood at the center of a pentagon of huge glass eyes, each three meters across, which afforded a complete view of the castle and the valley beyond. The Commander sat on his haunches on the throne, speaking to someone on a portable radio communicator set. The Commander's eyes rolled back to watch Turkey and Icehall enter the room.

(Speak no more, Custiss, whilst I am silent. Lowest of the Low hast returned, and the Star-Burner mechanic is with him. I smell the reek of plans gone awry.) The Commander left the throne and stood facing them on his hind legs. It was a posture of command and challenge that was lost on Icehall. (Account for thyself, wretch! Where hast thou been, and doing what?)

Turkey took several steps forward, hesitated, then stood on his own hind legs, and directed his claws forward.

The Commander's eyes widened and his jaw dropped for a moment. Then, fury: (Grovel, filth! How darest thou take that stance before *me*? Grovel, I command thee on this Day of Fire, and tell what thou doest!)

Turkey maintained his stance. (Three hundred years have I been filth. No longer! I come to reason with you, as an equal, or—)

(Equal! Reason!) The Commander was livid. (I have no equal and hear no reason but mine own!)

Turkey continued through the outburst. (—I come to challenge you, my Father.)

There passed a long silence. The two Rockchompers stood like statues in black stone, eyes locked.

(Thou comest, then, to claim thy birthright? Thou art premature; I yet live.)

(Nay, Father. I come to denounce the Day of Fire. As each peasant and noble must endure a foolish childhood unaware of its foolishness, so have we endured our childhood as a race. The world is bigger than this valley, and the universe far bigger than this world! We have met the gods and learned of the community of gods. We can be children no longer.)

(Gods! Madness! They are clever worms, not even fit to eat!)

(Beware these worms, O Father. In the sky circles the machine they ride in, a machine greater by five than Castle Harder-Than-the-Midnight-Sky, a machine that in seconds could turn us to bitter ash. The peoples of the sky deal by cooperation and free trade. We must meet them on their own terms.)

(I shall meet them only to conquer and enslave them!)

(Then I and thou and all our race will perish. Shouldst thou hurt even one of the Star-Burners, a thousand more will come, and all the world will flash to nothingness at their command. Heed me, Father!)

(Heed you! I command you, heed thy oath which thou swore whenst thou crawled from the Cauldron of Kings. The Day of Fire is upon us! Heed thy oath, lest it eat thy heart for thy defiance! Heed it, and be subject to me!)

Turkey stood firm. (The Star-Burners have an aphorism: 'There be no fool like an old fool.' Thou art fool, so bear witness that I break my oath! I give over my birthright and spit unhardened phlegm at thy feet! I shall be one with the Star-Burners as long I have wished, and I shall ride back to the stars with them when thou and thine are but ashes!)

The Commander broke his stance, threw back his huge stone-grey head, and roared. It echoed in the throne room and made Icehall's stomach turn. The raging Rockchomper leapt back to the throne and grasped two iron weapons from a rack. One he threw at Turkey hilt-first. Turkey grasped the weapon and took up guarded stance.

The Commander's eyes glittered. (Filth! Unnamed scum! I deny your fathering and ungive you my heritage! *Guard thy belly, bastard!*)

The Commander charged. He held his weapon teeth up, and raked it savagely back and forth as he ran. Turkey crouched, then sprang to one side as the Commander passed, simultaneously bringing the butt of his weapon down on top of the Commander's blade. Iron struck sparks on the stone floor. Turkey then brought his own blade up at the Commander's throat and missed as the older Rockchomper flattened himself out on the floor. The crouch was momentary. The Commander thrust his weapon between Turkey's hind legs and brought it upward and quickly forward. Turkey's dodge was not graceful; he leapt upward and backward, stumbling, with a grunt that Icehall knew was not speech.

The blades were saws, and fought as saws. Each tooth was itself a razor-honed hooked knife three centimeters long. One swipe with such a weapon would cut a man in half. Three swipes would part even a Rockchomper's rugged hide.

Icehall watched the ballet, terrified. When padding down a stone hall on all fours, the Rockchompers reminded him of bumptious, outsized dogs. Fighting on their hind legs with two-meter saws, they were devils out of Hell. The outlook for Turkey was not good, and Icehall could see no avenue of escape for himself.

The castle now shook continuously from the shifting of the valley floor. Icehall crept up against the shadowed wall beneath one of the enormous circular windows that were the Mouthless One's "eyes." He couldn't tell—yet—if the windows could be opened, but he reflected that he had a screwdriver and plenty of motivation.

The fight went on. Turkey was barely keeping himself from getting cut into chunks. A damned-fool courageous manic he might be; a seasoned saw-fighter he obviously was not. The Commander was playing with him. Turkey was being steered around the throne room for the Commander's entertainment, made to dance as a preface to the final killing slash that the Commander obviously had in waiting.

Something was happening outside. Over the rolling chaos of the shaking ground came a series of sharp concussions, ending with a single explosion that shook Icehall's molars. The sound of breaking stone and more explosions mingled with an evil subsonic grate like two continents dragged one over the other.

Icehall was thrown on his face as the floor of the throne room heaved up at a thirty-degree angle. He turned his head to see Turkey in mid-leap coming down atop the Commander, claws bared and sword raking. The Commander, disoriented by the heaving of the castle, scrambled away from his attacker. Turkey's raking thrust missed its target in the Commander's side, but came down hard on the middle of the Commander's whipping tail. The grate of sawteeth on bone was sickening, and Icehall saw two meters of the Commander's tail roll away across the tilted room, gushing deep maroon blood and twitching throughout its length.

The Commander wailed, inhaled, and screeched. Icehall had never heard a Rockchomper make such a sound; he longed to cover his ears. Then the bronze doors burst open, and the guards charged in, weapons ready.

At last Turkey found some discretion in his mad valor. With a ten-meter running start, he leapt over Icehall and through the faceted green glass window. Icehall swept shards of glass from his faceplate and saw a wounded Commander and three guards charging directly at him. He stood and started scrambling over the copper sill when a black snake with a trowel instead of a head struck him on top of the helmet. He grasped the tail, yelled, "Heave, dammit!" and closed his eyes.

10.
THE DAY OF FIRE

The top of the Mouthless One's head was wide and fairly flat. This was fortunate; the ground was continually shifting and shaking, and Castle Alpha rarely kept its attitude for more than a few seconds. Each of the glass eyes of the Mouthless One was surrounded by a ring of hornlike stone projections. Icehall and Turkey clung to the projections above the broken eye. Twice a guard from the throne room thrust his head through the broken glass; twice Turkey let him have the butt end of his weapon atop the head. It was a standoff that could not last. Icehall knew he should be thinking of escape, but could not.

Below and beyond them, the Day of Fire was blossoming.

Running along an erratic path down the center of the valley was a river of yellow-orange, pooling here and there in lakes of molten rock. Yellow-hot magma fountained skyward from the crack and splashed upon the darker rocks, running and streaming dull red back to the central mass. The continuous explosions sent lava bombs flying in all directions. Clouds of noxious gas, lit like demons by the glowing magma, writhed in the rising hot wind.

As they watched, the lava stream grew wider. The valley was filling. It was less than a kilometer from the base of Castle Alpha.

Several kilometers down the valley, the nearest other castle was now surrounded by molten rock. Icehall shielded his eyes from the glare. Tiny Rockchomper figures were unfurling four gigantic sails and rigging them. The sails glinted with a familiar ruddy gleam. Icehall was soon certain that they were forged of copper chain mail; cloth sails would burst into flame instantly in the firestorm. Each sail was painted with the figure of a black crucible pouring a stream of orange flame.

The lava was soon lapping at the base of Castle Alpha. A fierce hot wind was making Icehall very uncomfortable from temperature considerations alone. If even a small lava bomb flew his way he was a goner. His skintights were permeable and sweat-cooled; under molten rock they would melt like butter.

Motion caught his eye. Icehall looked downvalley. Castle Crucible was turning before the wind! The glow from the molten ocean made the stone bow appear to be awash in flame. The copper sails billowed, whipped, and filled. A yellow-hot spray blew to either side of the bow as the castle surged forward, underway on a broad lava river that was rapidly becoming a sea.

A lava bomb struck the side of the Keep with a splattering concussion. Icehall peered down and saw deep red viscous rock oozing along one of the Mouthless One's many legs, hardening as it ran. That was too close for him.

"I wouldn't send a dog out on a night like this," Turkey muttered.

"Hey, I gotta get off this thing and under cover. The heat's going to get me even if the molten artillery doesn't." Icehall peered backward and downward along the Mouthless One's flat skull. At least a dozen flared holes punctured the rock, some of which belched black smoke. "Hey, Turkey, could we get back inside down one of your chimneys?"

"Harrumph! Lemme see." Turkey inched his way backward and stared down a puckered elliptical opening perhaps a meter by two. "Kitchen vent. You game?"

"I'll go anywhere you'll go, brother." Icehall hooked his legs around a small vent pipe.

"Hokay! Don't touch that dial!"

Turkey scrambled further backwards along the idol's head, picking his way among the vent pipes. Icehall watched him stop, and incongruously lick the bottoms of both feet and his front hands. From that point on the way approached vertical, but Turkey crept down the stone like a fly, ripping one foot free and pressing another down tight.

He reached the shoulder of one of the Mouthless One's four sculpted metal arms and continued up the arm, pausing only occasionally to renew the stickum on the pads of his feet. Gripped in the idol's four hands were enormous blocks and tackle, each with a large coil of stiff grey cable. Turkey parted the coil from its pulley-block with one snap of his jaw, and wound the coil around his neck. Even while he climbed back up the side of the idol's head, Turkey was tying a loop in one end of the cable with his tongue-hands.

The chaotic pitching of the tortured valley floor had banked to a rhythmic rocking. Icehall realized that Castle Alpha was now afloat. Moments later, an unmistakable sound cut through the constant roar of the volcanic eruption: *J. Edgar Hoover*'s turbines revving to ignition speed, and then the staccato report and rising burble of the fusion tube igniting and coming to captive life. A blue-white glow from the fusion tube lit the tormented clouds for what must have been kilometers down the valley. Icehall wondered what the inhabitants of Castle Crucible and the others made of this new, painfully bright light. He wondered himself what madness had possessed Custiss to arrange such a travesty, and what the man intended to gain by it.

Slowly Castle Alpha was turning, rocking, coming about to face Castle Crucible. The wind was against them, but that didn't matter anymore; the fusion tube was better than any set of sails. Icehall was imagining new torments to inflict upon Custiss when Turkey returned, dangling a lopsided noose in front of his face.

"Down the hatch," the Rockchomper directed. Icehall gulped and nodded. He settled himself into the loop and allowed

Turkey to belay him down into the sooty pipe. Icehall kept himself clear of the pipe wall with his toes, kicking up clouds of clinging black dust as he went.

"Hey, how you gonna get down?" he yelled up the tube.

"Up on the housetop, click, click, click," Turkey's booming reply echoed down to him.

It was a long flue. Tributary pipes opened into it here and there, but Icehall's helmet lamp showed none of them to be large enough to admit either himself or Turkey. Icehall finally found himself standing on a flat metal surface about three meters square. It puzzled him until he realized that it was a griddle, Rockchomper-sized. The kitchen was dark and empty. Icehall gave the loop three sharp tugs and disentangled himself from it. The fibrous cable fell in stiff coils by his side. Ten minutes later, after much shuffling from above and falling soot, Turkey stood by Icehall's side and rolled his eyes. "Piece of cake," Turkey said. "Whew! Whillickers."

The pair picked their way through a rubbish-strewn, utterly dark corridor and emerged into the dining hall where they had demonstrated Boddkluskew's Black Widow device only the day before. Icehall's heart raced, and he swung his lamp around to the corner where he had left the magnificent Rabinowicz armored pressure suit. It was still there, leaning against the wall like a mummified corpse.

Getting into the suit was no problem. Icehall kept his skintights, and when the time came to swap helmets he kept his eyes shut and held his breath for the few seconds that the Rabinowicz life-support system needed to flush the bulk of the Scattershot air from the suit. The atmosphere held lots of very stinky things but nothing instantly lethal or particularly corrosive. Icehall was too delighted to be in a real armored, heavily insulated and temperature-controlled suit to object to some lingering chemical reek.

In the Rabinowicz suit belt there were tools, but nothing like a weapon a Rockchomper would understand. Icehall shrugged and made the helmet extrude a decimeter of slimjim and chased the meat with one of its three flavors of iced coffee. It was an *expensive* suit.

Icehall scanned the shuttle's comm frequencies until he found one in use. The Commander and Custiss were grinding and grating to each other. Breaking in would do no good. He made one attempt to contact Haatchtekfaaz directly on the bridge of the *Nixon*. The ship's computer would answer if it heard him; evidently the rock above them absorbed the signal.

"We're on our own. Hey, Turkey, what's he saying?" Icehall switched comm output to an external speaker. The Commander was shouting a single command at the top of his lungs.

Turkey yelped in alarm. "Man oh man! 'RAM! RAM! RAM! RAM!' D-Day! Remember the Maine!" Turkey shot off into the dark, Icehall stumbling along behind.

All the way to the main deck Icehall felt the acceleration of the shuttle's fusion tube. The bow of Castle Alpha was riding high by at least twenty degrees. Turkey and Icehall took side-tunnels and kept to the shadows, not wishing to meet any of the Commander's guards. Turkey heaved an iron manhole cover up and out of the way as they emerged onto the castle's deck mere seconds before impact. Off the bow was another castle, ablaze with torches, copper sails billowing. Then Castle Alpha's ram slammed into the side of Castle Crucible.

Icehall was thrown against a stone pillar as the deck heaved up. Oddly, there was little sound, but he felt through the soles of his boots the grinding of rock against rock, at last becoming the tumble of stone crumbling.

Castle Crucible rebounded from the impact. After a few minutes the two castles had drifted far enough apart for Icehall to see the damage. A tremendous crack had opened amidships of the other castle, widening as they watched. Without warning its entire bow crumbled and slid into the fiery morass. Almost simultaneously the crack became a gulf, and Castle Crucible split in two and capsized.

Icehall wanted to be sick. He watched hundreds of Rockchompers slide into the lava as the two remaining fragments of the castle turned bottom-up and rolled over. If any crew survived within the debris they were trapped, and the molten rock flooding through the stony corridors would be the end of them.

It took a few minutes for Icehall to recover his composure. "Come on. We're gonna put a stop to this."

The two picked their way through the forest of stone legs to the stern, where the cemented shuttle was again firing its fusion tube. The Rockchomper guard remained in an implacable ring around it. Icehall considered the situation long and well, and carefully measured the distance to the emergency hatch in *J. Edgar's* midsection via helmet radar. The helmet computer told him it was close enough.

"Let me stand on your shoulders, and then get up on your hind legs. I need a two-meter jumping start."

Turkey hunkered down and let Icehall climb to his shoulders. Icehall programmed the Rabinowicz's hydraulic knees with a few terse words to the helmet computer.

"Suppose you blow it?" Turkey asked.

"Use your imagination," Icehall replied, and jumped.

He hit the ground feet flat down so hard his arches stung, and let his knees flex fully. When they straightened on the rebound, it was with a powerful pulse from the hydraulic assist units, which carried him ten full meters, landing him squarely in front of a startled Rockchomper guard. The next leap was directed more upward than forward, over the line of guards, directly onto the hull of the horizontal shuttle. Icehall hit the hull metal hard and fell heavily on one shoulder. There hadn't been nearly enough time to practice.

The guards were befuddled for a second or two. Icehall scrambled a few meters up the hull on his hands and knees, and nearly tore a ligament heaving down on the emergency dorsal hatch release. The hatch flew up and open. Icehall glanced around. Somebody was throwing sizeable rocks at the Rockchomper guards. Good. Icehall slid into the airlock and stabbed at the button for automatic close-and-cycle.

The hatch began to close. It had only two decimeters to go when the black iron shaft of a Rockchomper weapon chunged in between hatch and hull. The hatch bit down on the weapon, ground for a moment, and halted.

"Now who's been giving them lessons!" Icehall fumed under his breath. He knew who, and it was an interesting problem. There was a way to blow the inner hatch without closing the outer hatch, and it would serve Custiss right. That, though, would take time. Icehall sat down in front of the control board and, tongue between teeth, began tapping in a long numeric code.

A noise from above made Icehall look up. He yelped. A Rockchomper was pulling the hatch open against the full force of its powerful hydraulic mechanism. Icehall watched several red lamps light on the panel, informing him that the hinges were giving out. Three more Rockchompers joined their fellow in the tug of war, and with a groaning crunch the hatch disappeared into the night.

A large Rockchomper head thrust down into the narrow airlock tube. Icehall punched it in the nose. It was like hitting a stone statue. The creature opened its mouth and wrapped Icehall in its tongue-hands. Icehall was dragged out of the airlock and away from the shuttle. He hung from the guard's tongue for what he thought was a long time. Somebody, somewhere, bounced a dozen good-sized rocks off the top of the guard's head, but the guard ignored the harassment.

Icehall supposed that the guards had sent a runner to inquire what to do with their prisoner. The answer, when it came back, was most unsatisfactory: The guard trundled Icehall over to the castle's edge, and pitched him out into the fiery gloom.

11.
BREAST STROKE

There was no time to swear. Icehall twisted around in his headlong plunge and aimed his right arm where he thought the side of the castle was. He clenched his fist hard, and *pfrroww!* went the Black Widow Worker Autoretrieval Device. He heard the adhesive capsule impact close by, felt the cord go taut—and felt the cord snap back at him. The adhesive had failed.

With a grim breath Icehall realized that he had used one cartridge already, in demonstrating the device during the welcome feast. Down below was molten red-orange doom. He clenched his fist again. *Pffffrroww-thwackkk!* The roiling lava was scant meters below him.

"Ufff!" he puffed as the cord went taut—and held. He spun wildly around an axis through his navel, and heard all three refrigeration units in the Rabinowicz energize at once. Everywhere around him was an orange-yellow glare upon whipping clouds of gas. The side of the castle was nowhere in sight. He was swinging like a plumb bob out to sternward, reached the extreme point of the swing, and started swinging back and down. Icehall craned his neck to see where he was heading, and screamed.

The low point of his swing was an easy two meters under the surface of the lava.

Icehall stabbed at the winch button. The winch took him up about a meter and jammed. A moment later he struck the molten rock.

The refrigeration units screeched. Icehall felt a flash of hell's heat over the entire length of his body. He watched gobbets of luminescent rock splash to one side, and felt the soft crunch of the partially-hardened surface layer giving way. Then he was free and swinging out to the opposite extreme of his pendulum oscillation.

The impact had robbed him of most of his momentum. He held his finger on the winch button, watched the winch suck in five more decimeters of cord, and jam again. He fretted as he reached the other end of his swing, paused, and wobbled back toward the low point.

Icehall felt the tug of new acceleration, and saw the blue-white glare of J. *Edgar*'s business end intensify far above him. The bow of Castle Alpha reared up. Icehall cleared the lava by decimeters, and swung far to the rear on his cord. His feet struck solid rock, but it was too smooth to afford any kind of grip. Quick thinking led him to kick hard, to give himself as much new momentum as possible.

The acceleration from the shuttle slacked off, and the bow fell. Once again, Icehall broke through the thin crust of hardened lava and sent up a spray of orange-hot molten rock before him. The refrigeration units howled for several seconds. Icehall shook crisp flakes of newly hardened rock from his arms and legs.

The suit spoke to him. "Three more temperature-change events of similar magnitude will result in permanent damage," the pleasant female voice said. "Five more will result in refrigeration unit failure. Please avoid such temperature-change events in the future, if possible. Thank you."

"You're welcome," Icehall muttered. He hit the winch with the flat of his hand. Half a meter of cord stuttered into its snout.

The bow reared again, enough to allow him to clear the lava on his backswing. Icehall gripped the winch with one hand and tried to haul up on the cord with his other hand, to give the winch motor some assistance. The winch ground sluggishly and took up a few more centimeters.

Icehall's hindquarters broke through the crust. He fanned flakes of rock from his rear, heard the suit scold him. He was scanning the cloud-shrouded side of Castle Alpha through the gloom, looking for a door, for a crevasse or handhold or anything to get him away from the ocean of molten rock. There was nothing.

Then a flit of motion high up in the distance caught his attention. Icehall craned his neck and watched a solitary Rockchomper figure arc out into the fiery night. He triggered his external speaker and hollered.

"Dammit, Turkey, this is no time to end it all! I'm all right!"

"Hark, hark, the lark!" echoed Turkey, just before he struck the molten rock and vanished in a shower of ruddy lava-gobbets.

Icehall cursed. The bow dipped low once more; he struck the lava hard. One of the three refrigeration units coughed and started cutting in and out. The inside of the suit was a steambath. Icehall wobbled slowly toward the opposite peak of his diminishing arc. The winch refused to budge. One more hit on the molten stuff would consume the last of his momentum and probably the remainder of his cooling machinery.

Icehall took a sip of cinnamon-hazelnut iced coffee and thought hard. In a water ocean there were icebergs. He looked for masses of floating rock to cling to. Anything was better than being dipped in and out of the lava like a teabag as Castle Alpha's stern rose and fell. A dozen meters to one side he saw a small lump of rock, and started calculating how he might reach it. Then he squinted, blinked, and looked again with his mouth gaping.

The rock had eyes. And it was swimming right toward him.

Icehall was speechless. Cutting a wake through the lava was his friend, mouth tightly shut and eyes hooded. Turkey was considerably less dense than the molten rock, so his body rode high. His front hands were tightly balled, fingers curled against palms, pushing lava to the rear in a power breast stroke.

Turkey swam to the point where Icehall was about to impact the molten rock. Icehall got the idea. His rump connected with Turkey's back. Two quick twists unhooked the winch from its harness. Icehall rolled over and wrapped both arms around the stout neck. Turkey thrashed his way toward Castle Alpha, keeping his head and upper back high out of the molten rock.

Thirty meters sternward along the wall of the castle they found the ramp that spiraled all the way from the deck to the base. Turkey pulled himself out of the lava, climbed a dozen steps, and collapsed.

"Ain't no picnic," he puffed. Icehall scrambled off his friend's back. He knocked crusts of faintly-glowing rock from Turkey's sides and legs. The fibrous scales that formed a Rockchomper hide looked undamaged; if anything, they seemed thicker and more impenetrable than ever. What effect such a dunking had on a Rockchomper he couldn't begin to guess. That it had not been instantly fatal was miracle enough for one day.

A stiff wind whipped up a spray of deep-red embers that crunched under Icehall's boots. Great flat islands of darker red were forming in the lava, splitting and letting gouts of yellow seep up between the fragments. Two other castles were within view, but neither seemed to be moving in their direction. Icehall felt the fusion tube flare. Castle Alpha began to roll as it turned in pursuit. Their side of the castle was dipping lower into the lava.

Icehall and Turkey scrambled up the ramp, a torrent of molten rock dogging their heels. One full third of the way around the circumference of the castle and perhaps halfway up from the lava line to the deck, Turkey stopped.

There was an indentation in the grey stone wall. Icehall watched as Turkey brushed cinders and dust away with his tongue-hands. It was a Rockchomper-proportioned door, one meter wide and two high, thoroughly sealed around all four edges. An angular hieroglyph showed faintly at the center. Icehall pointed to it.

"'Employees Only'," Turkey translated. Then, without warning, the Rockchomper appeared to become violently ill. For a solid minute he gagged and sputtered, then vomited, straight at the door.

Icehall should have expected as much. He watched, a little queasily, as Turkey spread the brownish ichor around the edges of the indentation. At once, a thin line around the door's periphery began to steam and bubble. Turkey grinned and snapped the fingers of his tongue-hands. He dug his front claws into the uneven stone, braced his rear feet against the door, and pushed *hard*.

"Open sesame!!" Turkey bellowed. The door tipped backward and vanished into the castle with a thudding concussion. The pair scrambled through the portal into utter darkness.

Turkey seemed to know where he was going. Icehall tried to follow and ran into a wall. Cursing, he told his helmet to sensitize its visor to short infrared. The visor went marbly for a moment and cleared. Turkey was now a multicolored blur vanishing down a twisting tunnel. The rocks were outlined in rainbow hues, reflecting heat that entered through the portal. Icehall followed.

These were the real depths of Castle Alpha. The lowest third of the castle had to be solid rock, Icehall thought, for ballast. This, the middle third, appeared to be storage. There were no torches in the iron torch-stands, and here and there tools and ceramic jugs were heaped in disorderly piles. For long minutes they ran in the darkness, with only Turkey's infrared image to guide Icehall's feet. Then Turkey stopped.

The helmet-computer was throwing wavelength-isophotes up on Icehall's visor. Turkey was a violet harlequin breathing clouds of faint red. The isophotes writhed in the air and vanished between breaths. Turkey pointed with a yellow-orange front claw: The isophotes crowded together around a glow from somewhere ahead. Visible light.

"Stairway to heaven," Turkey explained. "What's the game plan, chief?"

They were at the very bottom of the central stairway. Icehall leaned back on the rock and shook his head. The castle heaved and rolled around them. He had expended their best shot at stopping the carnage. What to do? Fight forty Rockchomper guards barehanded? Hide? Assassinate the Commander?

Icehall heard a noise from higher up on the stairway. Turkey darted ahead and peered into the torchlit gloom. Instantly he turned and raced back down the hall, not pausing but manhandling Icehall up under one arm at a dead run. Turkey hauled Icehall through two nearby archways, then ducked under a very low tunnel mouth and pulled Icehall after him. From entirely too close came gruff grinding voices and the scrape of iron weapons being dragged on stone.

"They must have heard you pop the hatch," Icehall hissed. Turkey clunked him hard atop the helmet. Icehall shushed. A guard waddled by in the hall, sawblade making a racket on the floor. He did not even glance into the low, dark room in which they were hiding.

"Why didn't he look in here?" Icehall demanded.

"Women's quarters. Off limits. Pshaw! Avast! Crazy world, ain't it?"

"They'll carve that on our tombstones."

"What now, my love?"

Icehall rattled his fingers on the side of his helmet. A good question. The guards were now actively searching for them, though not, extraordinarily, in this obvious hiding place. To go topside was death. Icehall had used all three shots in Boddkluskew's erratic skyhook. He had no weapons at all, and only playground-class self-education in fighting. All he knew was his beloved shuttle…

"Turkey, listen up. That trick you used on the doorway—does it work on solid rock?"

"Heesh! Yea, verily. That's a big ten-roger." Turkey spat on the stone by their feet. A circle of sizzling froth arose, outlined on Icehall's visor in dancing infrared isophotes. After half a minute the froth crumbled away, leaving a pit and some pale white powder around it.

Icehall forced his elation back. "Okay. It's nutty as hell, but that's long since ceased to be an issue: *J. Edgar Hoover* has two emergency hatches, one dorsal, one ventral. I almost made it through the dorsal hatch. The ventral hatch is identical, two thirds of the way toward the prow, right now facing down flat against the rock. But if we could get underneath it, and if you could make that gooky rockeater stuff sizzle its way *up*…"

12.
MOTHER MOST AWESOME

Turkey was agitated, and would answer no questions. At the rear of the strange cubicle where they were hiding had been an opening into a low, narrow tunnel; it seemed little more than a pipe to Icehall. They had been following that tunnel now for several minutes, downward and rearward into the depths of the castle. Icehall was starting to worry again. They should have been heading upward, toward the deck. There were no guards in the small tunnels, nor torches, nor torch stands.

Turkey walked on all fours, with the end of his tail lifted into the air. Icehall did an uncomfortable duckwalk, bent over at the waist, holding the tip of Turkey's tail. The stone conducted the subaudible rumble of the fusion tube to the soles of Icehall's feet, and to his fingers each time he touched the wall. He kept waiting for the concussion that meant another doomed castle had been rammed, but nothing came. The Rockchompers elsewhere in the valley had learned their lesson quickly.

Icehall's back was in agony by the time Turkey stopped. Icehall looked past his friend's bulk and saw a faint flickering of ruddy light. Icehall gave the end of Turkey's tail a conspiratorial squeeze, and Turkey jumped. Icehall's mouth went dry. If a creature who had boldly challenged the Commander was nervous, Icehall decided there was cause to be terrified.

Icehall felt Turkey shiver down the length of his back, then stiffen and walk boldly forward. Icehall followed, still gripping the tail. The pair ducked under another meter-high archway into a cavernous, smoky room. A dozen pair of baleful Rockchomper eyes glared at Turkey. The occupants of the room were smaller, smoother, and meaner-looking than the warriors guarding the shuttle. They were Rockchomper females. All were gathered around an enormous polished black granite bowl at least twelve meters across and four high, elaborately carved and enlaid with jewels, bright copper, and silver.

Icehall glanced around. The sputtering torches lit urns and glass bottles, bowls and stone jugs piled in corners and stacked on shelves cut into the stone. A figure of the Mouthless One stood in another corner, carved from what seemed to be jade. Close by the black granite bowl was a niche cut into the wall, in which rested a life-size grey stone statue of a Rockchomper, in an attitude of death or deep sleep.

Icehall gulped. *Idols and altars and alchemy!*

One of the Rockchomper women stepped forward, and sat down on her haunches, claws sheathed, head erect. Turkey and she locked eyes for a long time. Finally she spoke. The voice was not as deep as a male's, but it was no less loud.

(Must thou play the fool even unto the very hour of thy ascent? Where is the skull of thy father?)

Icehall noticed the claws creeping from the sheaths in Turkey's fingers. Again, there was no place to run.

(My father yet lives.)

The woman let out a grating shriek, and stood on her hind legs. She spat on the stone in front of Turkey. A wisp of green smoke drifted from the spot.

(Scum! Wretch! Filth! Thou *darest* not approach the Cauldron of Kings!)

Turkey didn't flinch. (I have yet to probe the limits of what I will dare. Tempt me not.)

Icehall was cataloging the places he could reach in a single leap of his hydraulic knees. There were several shelves with empty sections. There seemed to be enough room in the niche behind the grey statue to admit him. The solidest shelter in a melee, he thought, might well be inside the black bowl.

(I fear thee not, foolish male, who must fight by saw and by knife. There is no shield from the weapon of a woman.) She spat again, and the plume of smoke rose more quickly from the gobbet of corrosive poison. (Thy life is forfeit, yet I would know what madness impelled thee here.)

(I have come to save the Cauldron of Kings from destruction.)

The woman laughed. (Indeed. Is that not mine own task? And what danger fear thee?)

(I fear the wrath of the Star-Burners.)

(Ha! And what does an angry Star-Burner do? Beat its tiny hands against the stone?)

(They could turn this world to ash.)

(Yea, thou art mad. There is no such power in the world.)

Turkey leaned forward, eyes pleading. (There are many worlds, and among them powers beyond our knowing. What will thy ignorant pride avail thee when the fire from the sky turns the stone to steam above you, and cooks thy flesh ere it make steam of thee as well? Wilt thou call out my name and beg my forgiveness?)

(Hush. Thou art raving. Nay, speak to me of the Star-Burners whom thou lovest. They are clever things. I would breed them, re-form their lifestuff, make of them a race that would not hide within glass bowls. The one thou bringest, is he thy pet? I would have him for mine own…)

The Rockchomper woman stepped past Turkey and looked Icehall up and down. Icehall edged a half-step back.

(Touch him not, scum! Or I shalt crush thy headstrong skull and mop the scullery with thy ugly brain!)

The woman laughed, and reached for Icehall with both tongue-hands. Icehall yelled.

And leapt.

Right into the enormous black granite bowl.

A tongue-hand brushed his ankle but found no hold. It took the accuracy from the leap. Icehall struck the edge of the bowl with a pained grunt. He heard Turkey yelling behind him: "Not there, you damned fool!" Pell-mell he slid forward, tumbling head over heels down the shallow slope. Rockchompers were screaming in the background, and Icehall got the worst impression he should have leapt in another direction. *Any* direction.

Then something grasped his ankle, and this time took firm hold. Icehall stopped his slide scant decimeters from what lay in the bottom of the bowl.

It was not a liquid, yet it heaved in waves and hummocks in directions independent of the movements of the castle around it. The surface was pale sea-green, moist, and glittering under the smoky light of the torches. Here and there across the surface were little pools of true liquid. While he watched, a bubble rose from beneath, broke surface, and vanished, leaving a smear of brown slime behind. It reminded Icehall of a vacuole operating within a single-celled creature. Clearly the green stuff in the bowl was alive.

The shuttle mechanic looked more closely. Something was moving beneath the surface of the protoplasmic pool. Icehall switched on a tight beam from his helmet light. The beam penetrated well below the green surface, where a dark, wide-eyed face looked at him—and blinked.

Icehall scanned the light back and forth. Drifting through the green ooze was a miniature Rockchomper, complete with tongue-hands and trowel-shaped tail. Its large eyes opened and closed, and it seemed to be grinning.

That was as close a look as Icehall got. Strong tongue-hands were hauling back on his legs. Soon he was back over the edge of the black bowl, cowering behind Turkey, who was standing in a posture of defiance while trembling throughout his body.

The circle of Rockchomper women was closing in.

(Slay me, and thou slayest the last hope of our race,) Turkey warned.

(Thou art a disease, and we shall burn thy remains.)

The leader-female again spat smoking ichor between Turkey's front legs. Turkey edged back against the black bowl.

(Slay thou no one, Daughter.) A new, strange voice had spoken. Icehall whipped around. The grey statue in its niche had lifted its head, and opened its eyes.

The leader-woman touched the tip of her nose to the floor. (Mother-Most-Awesome! Thou hast not spoken for many days!)

(I have had much to ponder. Close thy mouth; swallow thy poison. There is madness everywhere around us.)

Icehall gulped, understanding none of the exchange. The lids over the ancient Rockchomper's eyes were furrowed and half-shut, but the eyes beneath were bright. The great head swiveled his way. Icehall could hear the aged flesh crackle and creak. The eyelids rose slightly. Her mouth bent into a wrinkled smile.

"Come to me, Citizen of the Combine," said Mother-Most-Awesome, in flawless American.

Icehall stepped over Turkey's tail, and stood in front of the niche where she lay.

"You took a leap in the dark, Citizen. Do you understand what you saw?"

Icehall nodded. "One of your kind, unborn."

"Ahhh, if only it were that simple. Custiss, your insane countryman, gave us a box that speaks your language. It taught me your words, your culture, your history. Or enough of it, at least, to know that you have nothing like this." One tongue-hand pointed toward the granite bowl. "You have had kings, who have sons who become kings. Even if the sons are born lame, or stupid, or blind, they become kings. Each son is the son of one man and one woman. The genes combine by fate's whim, and the results are a king, good or bad.

"Your race has lived a blinding flash compared to our glowing ember. I estimate that our written records extend five million of your years into the past, and we had language another million years before that. You have given up kings for talking machines. We have had the time to ponder life and its sources. This stone bowl you leapt into: We call it the Cauldron of Kings. Our common people reproduce by the random fates. But that will not do for a King.

"If the Cauldron is empty and we see that we may soon need a King, all our citizens present their genes to us. Once in the Cauldron, we watch over them and give them what materials they need to live independently of a body. Cell by cell, chromosome by chromosome, the genetic entities compete. Victors fight on; the vanquished are devoured. When the battle is ended, there is but one set of genes, and the embryo assembles itself. Only the hardiest genes will have gone into its makeup. We know that our King will be the best that we can produce.

"Still, that is not enough. A king must be wise and knowledgeable. Knowledge is nothing more than a brain's weight of accumulated chemical patterns. We know how they may be preserved and absorbed by a developing individual. When an old King dies, his skull is opened, and his brain is dissolved in the Cauldron. When the new King emerges, he will know all that the old King knew.

"Yet in all of this there is a deadly flaw. Old habits and ways get endlessly reinforced, almost driven into the genetic structure of our race. For some traits, say, loyalty and obedience, this is a good thing; it takes great courage to survive the physical pain caused by treason or disobedience. Others…the carnage outside had a rational origin. Our civilization cannot build lasting states and structures; the lava washes them into flame and ash. So we defend our little castles as best we can. Over the eons defense turned to offense. We attack and destroy one another when the Day of Fire's madness rises out of the cracks of the world. It is easy to remember how; it is harder to recall why."

The old head bowed; her eyes closed for a moment.

When they opened again, they were looking at Turkey.

"There is one further refinement. A King must not become a martinet drunk on his own self-importance. Therefore, when a King-to-be crawls from the Cauldron at our bidding, he is crowned the fool of all fools, the servant of all servants, the Lowest of the Low."

Icehall's jaw dropped. "And if the Commander dies …"

"When, Citizen, when. When the Commander dies, your friend will become the Commander. Did he not share his destiny with you?"

Icehall felt a little dizzy. Turkey, then, had reasons of his own for wanting to leave Scattershot. The castle shuddered around them under the thrust of the shuttle's fusion tube. *Good* reasons.

(Mother-Most-Awesome!) Turkey rumbled, eyes on the stone between his feet. (We have not time for natural history! I beg of thee!)

(Hush, my child. If I must think faster than madness, I should be mad.) In American, she again spoke to Icehall. "You must see that all we have labored for these countless years lies in the Cauldron by your side. We here have sworn a truly deadly oath to die in its protection. I have seen the images of your machines and starcraft. I feel the rumbles of this thing my Eldest Son has glued to our afterdeck, the thing that is but a toy in your scheme. The energies you control are frightening. I do not doubt that any one of your starcraft could make ash of Castle Alpha.

"That much I read. The true soul of your people, however, I cannot. In your short history there have been heroism and barbarism, awesome devotion and bravery layered upon frightening treason, everywhere endless contradiction. I must know, Citizen: Should your lives here be forfeit, would your countrymen cause harm to the Cauldron of Kings?"

Icchall wasn't sure, but he doubted it. New, unconsolidated cultures were handled with reasonable care. This situation, however, was easy enough to read.

"We came here on a peaceful mission of trade, offering chances of mutual profit," he faked. "If we die…there would be little hope for you."

The great eyes closed again. When they opened, her head turned back toward Turkey.

(Lowest! Your plan, briefly and concisely!)

Turkey spoke for several minutes in his own language. A brisk, heated interchange followed among the women in the room. (Mother, that is insanity! Our task is here!)

(Thy task is to protect the Cauldron. Obey.)

(The madness of men! We should chain them to the rocks and forbid them these deadly games!)

(Without women there is no life; without men there is no destiny. Obey me, I say!)

(I cannot. Thy brain…has soured.)

The old head rose slightly. From between wrinkled lips shot a sizzling gobbet, which struck above the lintel of the only door into the room. (Thou may argue that my brain has soured. I show thee, my aim has not. Leave and obey the Lowest as though he had come unto his station, or never enter this portal alive again. Begone, all!)

13.

THE HALL OF SKULLS

Their destination was a tomb. Icehall followed Turkey into a circular hall a hundred meters in diameter. The females followed behind, each carrying a fat stone jug. Save for three torches carried by the females and one by Turkey, the hall was utterly dark.

The burble of the fusion tube was a nearly tactile presence, immediately above and before them. This was the rearmost room in the uppermost level of Castle Alpha. Icehall scanned the walls with his helmet beam. Hundreds of stone slabs two meters by three jut from the polished stone walls. Nearly all of them supported Rockchomper remains, tatters of shriveled hide stretched over massive bones below the trephined, grinning skulls. The slabs were stacked twenty high to the ceiling, thirty meters above. According to Turkey, a Commander could live for a thousand years, and here were the remains of a thousand Commanders.

"Get somebody to take the torches outside," Icehall told Turkey. One of the Rockchomper women complied, and they were in total darkness.

Icehall sensitized his visor to infrared, and looked toward the rear of the tomb. An oblong, irregular blotch showed in several colors upon the rearmost part of the ceiling. *J. Edgar Hoover* had been heating the rock for several hours. Icehall tuned the visor up and down the infrared spectrum, and watched wavelength isophotes warp and flow over the rock background. The outer shell of the shuttle was very well insulated from the inner structures, except near the ports. Those would show up as cooler spots, influenced by the shuttle's internal air conditioning.

The heat patterns were distorted by passage through the stone, but Icehall decided he saw a cooler smudge at eleven thousand angstroms.

"Two meters in from the wall, above the skull that's leaning toward the right," he directed.

"Ain't we got fun," Turkey commented in the dark. More torches were lit, and the real work began.

Hung with stone jugs, rope, hoses, and other peculiar things, Turkey clambered from slab to slab toward the ceiling, careful not to disturb the mummified remains. Once on the highest slab, he pointed from spot to spot on the ceiling until Icehall nodded assent. Icehall then watched him plug the hoses into the jug mouths and arrange a set of tubes and a bladder that seemed to be a pump. He raised a lumpy hammered-brass tube with two snouts and pointed it at the selected spot.

"Art steps in where nature fails," Turkey said, giggled, and squeezed the bladder hard. Twin streams of viscous fluid left the snouts and hit the ceiling.

The effect was explosive. Billows of yellow gas poured from the stone. Spatters of gritty, smoking mud flew everywhere. In moments Turkey was covered with it. He kept grinning and pumping the bladder. A hundred-kilo chunk worked loose from the ceiling and smashed to the floor. Dribbles of the fluid began eating into the floor, into the slabs near the ceiling, into everything, Icehall thought, but Turkey himself. Icehall took a few steps backward. This was not the time to put the Rabinowicz suit through a chemical torture test.

Turkey was following the hole he was burrowing, pulling back only to dodge the fragments loosened by the solvent. When one set of jugs emptied, he hauled another to the ceiling and began again. In time only the trowel-shaped end of his tail protruded from the hole, twitching and flipping back and forth. The women stood silent and unreadable on either side of

Icehall, watching the mud, smoke, and gas blow out of the hole. Icehall began to wonder what the stuff would do to hull metal.

Abruptly the storm of corrosives stopped. Turkey's tail drew up into the hole and vanished. Moments later, a tumble of hundred-kilo paving stones rolled out of the burrow and struck the floor. The sound of the fusion tube trebled. Then the frayed end of another Rockchomper rope danced its way out of the hole until it brushed the floor. A stentorian voice bellowed from above: "Awwwwwwllllll aboooooooooord!"

Icehall's heart was beating fast. He looped the rope through the defunct Black Widow harness and gave it three sharp tugs. Turkey hauled him up as though he were a sinker on a fishline. The walls of the burrow were still slimy and smoking faintly. Icehall scrunched up his shoulders to avoid brushing the stone.

The rock was over five meters thick. Turkey hauled him into the shallow empty space left by the paving stones from Castle Alpha's deck. Icehall bumped his head on *J. Edgar Hoover*'s underbelly and smiled: The groove for the central hatch release was square over the tunnel's mouth. One twist of the wrist brought the hatch down with a wheeze. Turkey tried to follow him into the airlock, and got as far as his massive shoulders.

"Mmph. It's been years since I fit into a ten," Turkey grumbled. Icehall rummaged through a cabinet in the lock and found a spare suit helmet. He switched it to his own helmet frequency and handed the helmet to his friend.

"We'll be in touch through this," he said. "Anything you say into the helmet will reach me. Now…where the devil did all that rockeater stuff come from?"

Turkey tucked the helmet into one cheek. "Don't ask. Just never get on the wrong side of a woman."

A tongue-hand squeezed Icehall's ankle, and the great head withdrew.

14.

"I HAVE BEEN ORDERED TO CATEGORICALLY DISOBEY YOU."

The lock cycled. Icehall was on his own, in his element. He looked up to the inner hatch of the emergency port and hesitated. So far, things had played entirely into Custiss's hands. The man had had some time to think his madness through. Caution was called for—and a good meal wouldn't hurt. "*J. Edgar*! Open inner hatch."

"I have been ordered to categorically disobey you," the shuttle replied.

"Like hell. Open the inner hatch!"

"I have been ordered to categorically disobey you," the shuttle insisted.

Categorically? Disobey? That was a new wrinkle in shuttle command management, and one that definitely smelled of university thinking. *J. Edgar Hoover* could be instructed to ignore commands from specific persons. "Categorical disobedience" had to be a Custiss invention; the man must have considered Icehall too dangerous to merely ignore. The concept was worth exploring.

"*J. Edgar Hoover*! Close the inner hatch!"

The computer sounded mildly offended. "Please clarify. The inner hatch is already closed."

"I don't care! Close that hatch and keep it closed!"

"The hatch *is* closed. I *am* keeping it closed."

"Do you hear me? I don't want an argument! Mind your orders. I am *categorically* ordering you to close that hatch and keep it closed no matter what anybody says! Do it!"

The shuttle took a moment to think it through. "This transaction has been logged under 'Irresolvable Contrarational Activity'," it said. The hatch slid open with a wheeze.

Icehall climbed up and through the hatch, laughing. "Open the hatch and keep it open!" he called over his shoulder. The hatch wheezed shut without an argument.

Icehall gratefully removed his helmet and scratched. A cold washrag and some rehydrated spaghetti further buoyed his spirits. He clamped a new recirculator tank onto the Rabinowicz. That done, he pulled the little radio console down from its stowed position. Just like taking candy from a baby.

"*J. Edgar*: Break my connection to *Nixon* and hang up on Mr. Haatchtekfaaz."

"I have been ordered to categorically disregard you."

"Whoops. Somebody's getting smart in his old age." Icehall tried to make a manual connection, but the console would not respond. Not good. Haatchtekfaaz had to hear what was going on.

Behind him, the fusion tube roared, suddenly at full throttle. Icehall gripped a stanchion. Moments later he was thrown to the floor. The grate of crumbling rock shook the shuttle. Had Castle Alpha been damaged? Icehall cursed and got to his feet.

"This has gotta stop."

Ten minutes later Icehall had half the floor plates pulled up, and was considering the circuitry running between the hulls. His heart was in his throat, and a live ion torch burned in the grip of his right hand. He had never deliberately damaged his shuttle before…

The fusion tube roared again. Icehall steadied himself, then grunted and got down to the dirty business. The torch bit into a two-inch aluminum bus bar, sizzled, brightened into a miniature nova as the plasma began to conduct. In less than a minute the bar melted through in a shower of aluminum droplets and a searing burst of yellow-green arc.

The shuttle's computer dropped dead for lack of power. The lights dimmed, then brightened as the stupid but reliable backup controller took over. The fusion tube went into standby. For several long minutes, the *J. Edgar Hoover* was very quiet.

Then the fusion tube coughed, vibrated heavily, and came back to life. Icehall shook his head in wonder as he heard the tube rev and fade, rev and fade, like the engine of a hotrod turbine racer.

There could be only one explanation: Custiss was controlling the fusion tube manually. In a series of ragged lurches the tube came back up to full thrust. Castle Alpha wobbled forward again, after new prey.

Icehall raged in frustration. He threw the still-smoking torch at a wall and kicked a loose floor plate across the cargo hold. Enough was enough. He was not a brawler, had never given anyone more than a bloody nose, and had agonized about that for weeks.

Behind the cargo hold's forward bulkhead was the life-support system. Icehall swung back a panel and swung up a small control console. He started tapping in commands. *J. Edgar* might have given him an argument, but the backup controller was anyone's slave. Further within the maze of pipes and hoses, valves were snapping open and shut, and several pumps were howling up to speed. Icehall looked grimly at the chronometer in the corner of his faceplate. Not long…

Icehall gathered what spare and emergency spacesuits he could find and tossed them in a pile behind him. That done, he manually set up the maser link to the *Nixon*.

"*Nixon*, this is Icehall on *J. Edgar Hoover*! Tell Haatchtekfaaz to get to the comm console!"

The pleasant baritone voice of *Nixon*'s computer answered. "I'm sorry, Mr. Icehall, but Mr. Haatchtekfaaz began his powered descent in the *John Mitchell* eight minutes ago. The *John Mitchell* has been fitted with the full Conflict Option Package. You should expect touchdown of the *Mitchell* in approximately nineteen minutes."

Nineteen minutes! And with the COP! Haatchtekfaaz was burning a hole in the sky! Icehall couldn't think of anything to say that would do the old Atrinite any good. Haatchtekfaaz was on his way, loaded for bear. Bear was what he was going to find. Bear, to the seventeenth power.

The pipes beyond the bulkhead roared for ten minutes before the intercom gleeped from the comm console. Icehall smiled, but there was a knot in his stomach.

"Icehall! What's going on back there? Cabin pressure is way down!"

Icehall cleared his throat and gulped. "I'm evacuating the air from the shuttle, Mr. Custiss. In fifty minutes you'll be breathing fair vacuum." Icehall heard the man mutter before the intercom switched off. The fusion tube went back into standby. Very soon after, Icehall heard hatches opening manually, heading aft.

Icehall picked up a five decimeter open-end wrench and stood to one side of the hatch, watching the emergency release twist. The door swung away, and a figure in an emergency suit bumbled through. Icehall brought the wrench down atop the suit helmet with a clang, realized the foolishness of that, and leapt full upon Custiss's back.

Instantly he found himself lying on the floor, gripping an empty, inflated spacesuit. Custiss stood in the hatchway, holding a hand tracton.

"You're an idiot, Icehall."

"Ouch. Takes one to know one."

"Turn off the purge. Now. Or I'll burn a hole in your suit."

Icehall shrugged and shut down the pumps, then released atmosphere from the reserve tanks to normalize pressure. Custiss waved him toward the forward hatch. "You're going outside again. The guards will be glad to see you."

Icehall hung back, shaking his head. "You really expect to get away with this. You think you can lock up an entire ship's crew, steal a shuttle, and commit mass homicide on an unconsolidated intelligent race. Chutzpah, Mr. Custiss, in spades. But that won't save your hide when this whole affair is over and they come looking for you."

Custiss grinned. "Let them look. Until this race is consolidated and a permanent trade mission is established, nobody's going to be sending troops down here. That could take months. The Commander has promised to keep anyone from finding me. Once the magma solidifies outside, the whole valley is going to be rotten with new lava caves. You could hide anything out there. And of course, when this Day of Fire is over, the Commander will be in charge of the entire valley. Nobody will find me if I don't want to be found."

Icehall shrugged. "Maybe. You know that the Combine will try to buy them off. Everyone has his price. Think about what the Commander might turn you in for. A few bulldozers. A dozen leaper platforms. If all else fails, weapons."

The thought seemed to trouble Custiss. He shook his head. "I don't think so. They're true primitives. Stubborn. Magnificently stubborn! Loyal, as well. Such crass treachery exists only in advanced capitalistic technological societies. The Rockchompers haven't been corrupted by either capitalism or technology yet."

Icehall kicked a nearby bulkhead. "Well, you're giving them a helluva head start. Is it worth it, Mr. Custiss? Really worth it?"

Custiss leaned forward, face intense. "Anthropologists do one of two things: They either teach anthropology to other anthropologists, or they spend their lives in front of terminals, sifting through other people's data for scraps. Once in a lifetime luck chose me to make the first study of a newly contacted and unconsolidated intelligent race. One in a *trillion* luck landed me here, alone, just before a Day of Fire. Fate handed me the chance to make the most outrageous anthropological experiment in history, something no one would ever do again. If you had been in my place, you would have leapt on it even faster than I did."

Icehall gulped. It was dangerous in the other fella's shoes. As a starship mechanic he himself was no stranger to the very human urge to tinker. He forced it out of his mind. "But the lives, think of all the intelligent lives you're taking! For nothing!"

"As though they wouldn't be taking those lives on their own, without my help! Don't think I haven't thought this through!"

"You—" Icehall began.

Both men stopped. Someone was beating on the outside of the hull with the butt of a weapon. Two more joined in, urgently.

"My god! I've wasted enough time talking!" Custiss ran to the comm console on the forward bulkhead and brought up an aft imager. He yelped, then turned and ran through the cast-wide hatch without a thought for Icehall.

Icehall found himself unable to turn away from the comm screen. It showed a castle bearing down on them, sails billowing, about to ram from behind. It was close. Every detail was clear, in the glare from the glowing magma all around: The whipping sails of beaten copper mail, the facet-eyed head of their own version of the Mouthless One, with flickering shadows playing among its many stone legs. Lined up upon the heaving bow were rank upon rank of Rockchompers, each holding a saw-bladed weapon at ready. Icehall could see the orange glint in their eyes. There was special vengeance on their minds for Castle Alpha, now that its fiery magic had failed.

Icehall swallowed hard. The fusion tube was still silent. Even if Custiss brought it up immediately, the enormous mass of Castle Alpha would prevent it from pulling away in time. Whatever happened, the ram would be within seconds.

"Turkey!" Icehall shouted into his helmet mike. "We're being rammed from behind! Get forward and down!"

That was all the warning Icehall could afford to offer his friend. For himself, there was now only one way out. He turned to the three-meter square cargo hatch. Icehall flipped a guarded red lever to one side. The webbing of the ejection cot popped out from a slot and hung in the air. Like a frantic spider Icehall grasped the hatch's handholds and pulled the webbing around his body. The hatch sensed his efforts and its emergency systems came to life.

"Leaper bottles, report!" Icehall shouted.

"Full charge!" they replied in unison, four strong.

"Battery, report!"

"Full charge!" the gruff canned voice said. Icehall thumbed another button. Four padded steel bands rotated out of the hatch and clamped his legs and torso in place. A small control panel extended and locked beside his right arm. A screen on the panel lit with an image of the chaos outside.

"Clamped tight and nominal!" the hatch declared.

"OK, then *blow!*"

The ragged report from forty explosive bolts deafened him and threw him against the steel bands with a painful wrench. Then the hatch was free and flying on the thrust from four leaper bottles built into the double wall.

Through the ringing in his ears Icehall heard the cavernous echo of the two castles colliding. Behind that sound came the continuous cacophony of crumbling rock as Castle Alpha's stern caved in.

Obeying commands from its meager AI, the hatch flipped over to put itself between Icehall and the shuttle. The system had been designed for rapid escape from a runaway fusion tube. The hatch's sensors had caught the first burst of neutrons from the reigniting tube. Icehall willed his vertigo away and shouted a command to the hatch to lock its screen on the shuttle.

Cables were being thrown from the attacking castle. Each one struck Castle Alpha and stuck on Rockchomper adhesive. Rockchomper boarders began inchworming across on the cables, weapons clamped in their jaws.

Then there was blinding light as the fusion tube caught and came up to full throttle. A cloud of white-hot plasma roared from *J. Edgar Hoover* and washed rearward over the deck of the attacking castle. Icehall's gorge rose to see the Rockchomper invaders catching fire and leaping into the ocean of lava like fallen angels thrown into Hell.

The shuttle continued to blast. By meters it drove the two castles apart. Anything that could burn on the attacking castle was blazing, its copper sails running molten over the stone deck like ruddy, glowing water.

With the invaders' bow removed from the ruins of Castle Alpha's stern, there was little left to support the stern and the roaring shuttle. Icehall watched cracks appear in the stone. Still Custiss kept the tube blazing at full throttle. Once, twice, the prone spacecraft lurched as stone gave way beneath it. Horrified, Icehall watched the shuttle break free of the afterdeck and launch itself upward and forward. Icehall blinked and looked again.

Hanging from *J. Edgar Hoover*'s lower surface were fifty tonnes of solid rock.

15.
THE DESCENT OF THE *JOHN MITCHELL*

The *J. Edgar Hoover* arrowed toward the sky at a thirty-degree angle, graceful steel half-buried in blackened stone. A heartbeat later it struck the side of the Mouthless One's head. The head and shoulders of the idol shattered into flying fragments that caromed off the idol's hundreds of legs and tumbled about on the deck. Icehall had a moment to think: *And now Turkey gets his promotion.*

The hatch had flown high and clear of Castle Alpha to protect Icehall from the shuttle's deadly exhaust. Still locked on the shuttle, the hatch's screen showed the blazing tail reaching higher and higher into the murky sky. Icehall knew Custiss was trying to make orbit. Orbit was his last chance; not even a miracle would land the shuttle and its halo of rock again.

J. Edgar Hoover was now a blazing torch in the night sky, painful white with an aura of violet. Icehall soon saw that its path was not a solid orbital insertion trajectory, but rather a flattening arc. The computer might have had a fighting chance of orbiting such a heavy, lopsided mass; Custiss the anthropologist had no such skill.

The arc flattened, and curved ever more rapidly back down toward the valley. Indistinctly through the wavering, tormented air, Icehall saw the shuttle throw up a huge curtain of lava as it struck under full throttle, followed by a searing spherical bubble of plasma as the fusion tube went critical and died.

Half a minute later the shockwave reached Icehall, and he felt the metal of the hatch tremble. "Hatch, bring us back to an inconspicuous place on the deck of the Castle. And please make it the *right* Castle."

The hatch set down in the shadows behind the ruined Keep, concave side downward, leaving Icehall hanging in the embrace of the four steel bands. He forced himself to take a long sip of iced coffee and think.

He did not think for long. Abruptly a Rockchomper leapt up atop the hatch and began bellowing in that furious, imperative tone the Commander had used during his battle with Turkey in the idol's head. Could the Commander have somehow escaped the ruin of the Mouthless One? Icehall began to shake. Then a familiar rhythm rapped out on the metal above him: Dut-dududut-dut...dut-dut!

"Talk about relief! Hatch, let go!"

The bands contracted back into the hatch, dropping Icehall into the embrace of the webbing. As quickly as he could he crawled from beneath the hatch. "Turkey..."

But it could not be Turkey. The Rockchomper standing atop the hatch was too tall, too thickly muscled, too perfectly in control of his aspect. He held a huge toothed sword in one front hand. All his claws were fully extended, and glinted midnight black in the light of wind-whipped torches.

Standing in a circle all around them were thirty of the Commander's guard, weapons ready. Icehall thought about crawling back under the hatch.

At a sharp, deep syllable, the guards prostrated themselves on the stone. They were making obeisance to...

"Commander!" Icehall said. This Rockchomper's tail was whole and uninjured.

Turkey whipped around, startled. "Arrgh! Et tu, Icehall? Jeez! Mercy! I liked my other handle better, 10-4."

"Turkey! Damn! I thought you were a goner!" Icehall leapt up on the hatch and playfully clonked his friend atop the head. The guards began to grumble.

(What manner of worm may strike the pate of the Commander and live?)

Turkey whirled around and brought the butt of his weapon down hard on the grumbler's crown. (Swallowest thou whole the stone that thou knowest not how to chew.)

Several of the other guards laughed. Turkey relaxed; Icehall saw the old grin returning to that stony face.

"Zut alors! Yowza! On the whole, I'd rather be in Philadelphia."

(Commander! Behold the welkin! Yet another burning star!)

Turkey and Icehall looked skyward. A blue-white point was becoming a painful blaze, arrowing down from the west.

"Guess who's coming to dinner?" Turkey said, looking to Icehall for guidance.

"Lordy. I forgot about old Hatchet Face. Get your people off the deck. He's coming down fast, hot, and angry. *Nixon* told me that he figured out the situation down here. He's fitted the other shuttle out with armor and some pretty gawdawful firepower. Let me calm him down. He'll be gunning for the Commander, so whatever happens, *you* stay out of sight!"

"Roger dodger! Jeepers creepers! It's a hot time in the old town tonight!"

Turkey leapt off into the shadows, bellowing orders to his guards.

Icehall peered into the molten night. The other castles were keeping their distance. The magma itself was cooling from orange to a very dull red, drifted widely with floating islands of black. This Day of Fire was ending.

From above, the *John Mitchell* was now casting a shadow. Icehall scrambled down on his stomach and crawled beneath the hatch. There was no better radiation shielding within reach. Blinding white light crept under the hatch and darkened his faceplate, while the burbling thunder of a fusion tube descending rattled the hatch against the stone. Abruptly the light and sound ceased.

Some minutes later Icehall emerged. A hundred meters away stood the *John Mitchell* on its vertical struts, fitted with a Conflict Option Package. The craft was surrounded by a perfectly reflecting cylinder interrupted by six equally-spaced transparent bubbles. Behind each bubble was a supercooled coleostat capable of steering the beam from one of the six petawatt tractons embedded in the armor cylinder.

The stone under the shuttle was still glowing yellow-hot. A thunderous, scratchy (if slightly squeaky) voice echoed from the shuttle: "I SPEAK WITH THE AUTHORITY OF THE PEACEKEEPING COMMITTEE OF THE TRIPARTISAN ECONOMIC COMBINE! RELEASE YOUR COMBINE CITIZEN PRISONERS!"

Icehall was trying frequency after frequency.

"Haatchtekfaaz! Lay off! Everything's all right! Do you read me? Turn your radio on, dammit!"

"I AM EMPOWERED TO TAKE DRASTIC ACTION!"

"Haatchtekfaaz! Do you read me? Pick it up already!"

"RELEASE YOUR PRISONERS!"

Icehall started to trot toward the shuttle. He paused when he noticed one of the coleostats swinging down from its rest position.

Kraaaaaaaak!

A sizzling blue-hot beam swept out a ninety-degree arc twenty meters away from the shuttle. Icehall dove again for the shadows. For a moment there was new lava spattered into the air. The groove cut by the beam faded slowly from yellow-hot, and smoked.

Icehall sat behind one of the Mouthless One's many legs, wishing he could chew his fingernails. Nothing happened for twenty minutes.

Given what Icehall knew of Haatchtekfaaz, the old Atrinite's next move was not unexpected. A spindly scarecrow figure covered with mirror-bright reflecting armor dropped from the narrow gap between the shuttle and its armor sheath. Haatchtekfaaz was wearing a beam-armored Manplifier Mark IX suit with full power assist on all joints. He could easily jump ten meters straight up if he had to.

Haatchtekfaaz stalked from the shuttle's shadow, carrying a husky tracton rifle. He paused every few meters to peer into the moonlit gloom.

Icehall had seen enough. Again he left shelter and ran toward the Atrinite, waving his arms and yelling.

Haatchtekfaaz turned toward Icehall. Moments later, a ten-kilo rock flew from the shadows and struck the hydraulic machinery covering Haatchtekfaaz's right arm. The tracton rifle spun off and clattered on the stone. Haatchtekfaaz pitched over backwards from the force of the blow.

From among the Mouthless One's many legs came a bellow; a familiar, frightening sound. A furious Rockchomper with a foreshortened tail was loping toward Haatchtekfaaz with front hands outstretched, claws bared and raking the air. He seemed intent on tearing the old Atrinite apart.

(Death to all Star-Burners and their *klitchromp*-eating machines!)

Haatchtekfaaz, stunned, was trying to get his hydraulic legs beneath him again. Icehall dashed for the tracton rifle, still twenty yards away. Even the thought of a tracton in his hands was little comfort. *I could slice him into fifty pieces and still be afraid of the pieces!*

Icehall leapt the last ten meters on his powered knees, rolled over twice, picked up the rifle and fell into a crouch. He drew a bead on the advancing Commander and pulled the trigger. The rifle's battery pack sizzled and spat molten metal in all directions. Then: "Geronimo!"

From off to his right, another familiar figure was galloping his way on all fours. While still twenty meters from the furious Commander, Turkey arched his back and drew his tail up tightly behind him. Scarcely breaking his running pace, Turkey defecated on the trowel-shaped tip of his tail.

In one smooth motion, Turkey raised his tail over his head and whip-cracked it in a tight circle. The dollop of slime arced forward into the Commander's path and splashed on the stone. The Commander set one clawed hind foot in the puddle and fell heavily on his face.

Turkey followed the glue with a hefty mouthful of Rockchomper hardener. The greenish saliva splattered on the Commander and the puddle of glue, sizzling where it reacted. The Commander threw his back into a powerful spasm to rise and flee, but it was too late. All four limbs and his lower jaw were glued tightly to the stone.

Turkey trotted up to the fallen Commander and sat down on his haunches. The Commander glared poisonously at him. Turkey didn't even blink.

"Stick around, Pops. I got a *bone* to pick with you!"

16.

LEAVETAKING

It was a noisy departure for the crew of the *Richard M. Nixon.* Two tonnes of the finest glue in known space had followed Boddkluskew and Captain Bend-Waugh back to safety on the *Nixon*, where each had vowed never to have anything more to do with unconsolidated aliens as long as he lived. Icehall was girding himself for six weeks of continuous I-told-you-so's from Haatchtekfaaz, to which he could only think to reply: *Hey, it's a living…*

He would face that as it came. For the moment, Icehall lingered on the cargo porch of the *John Mitchell*, now bereft of armor and weaponry, while Turkey stood beside him and thundered to the gathered crowds in their own grating language.

Repairs to the Keep were well underway. It would be harder to fix the stern, but the Rockchompers would doubtless find a way. New cultures often took years to melt into the mainstream of the Tripartisan Economic Combine, but by the time the next Day of Fire rolled around, Icehall felt certain the peoples of Castle Valley would be far too busy making money to sail their stone firejammers to war again.

Turkey's departure was a larger festival than any in living memory. The guards had polished their saws and stood rank upon rank in front of the Commander, who glared at the ground between his feet, his shortened tail crisscrossed with fibrous Rockchomper bandages. To Turkey's right the female priesthood stood in a circle about the reclining figure of Mother-Most-Awesome, and in Mother's front arms was cradled a tiny Rockchomper, no more than a meter long. The little creature was chattering and waving a yellow banner in the air. All around them, standing, sitting, making signs in the air with their tongue-hands and grating their farewells, were the common folk of Castle Alpha. Icehall sensed more relief than regret in their gestures and words.

Turkey was milking the occasion for all it was worth.

(… so let it not be said I pass away from thee without legacy! I leave thee a promise, and a warning: Ignorance and ancient habit chain us to this valley, but by my word, the friendship of the peoples of the Stars will make all this world ours to cherish, and a thousand other worlds ours to share and explore. But should we accept the gifts from the stars and cling to our violent heritage, there will soon be none alive to reap the boon. For anger merges with energy to become the disease that is its own cure. I pray thee all, seek wisdom and reason, and the Stars shall be thine forever!)

Pandemonium followed; the crowds seemed genuinely moved. Icehall watched, amazed, as the newborn Lowest of the Low leapt from the ancient arms of his protectress and skittered across the stone to the ladder of the shuttle. The little being clambered up the rungs as though born in the act, and thrust his banner into Turkey's proffered hand.

"Take…a…long…walk…off…a…short…plank!" the tiny creature squeaked, then giggled, and spat in Turkey's face.

"Must have gotten it from his mother's side," Turkey muttered, and followed Icehall's laughter into the shuttle.

AUTHOR'S AFTERWORD

This story sat in a box for most of 35 years, and thereby hangs a tale. In 1977, I had begun selling short stories to editor George Scithers at *Isaac Asimov's Science Fiction Magazine* (IASFM). George was very encouraging, and late that year told me that he and his publisher were launching a new magazine, *Isaac Asimov's SF Adventure Magazine*. He was looking for space adventure stories reminiscent of the better pulps like the long-defunct *Planet Stories*, and accessible to younger readers. He invited me to submit stories in that subgenre, if I had any.

I did. In fact, in high school I had taken notes on a concept for a race of heavily-insulated aliens called "Rockchompers" who ate rocks, and sailed stone ships on an ocean of molten lava. It sounded like just the thing. I told it from the point of view of a young shuttle pilot, as a nod to the magazine's targeted younger readers. I started in early 1978. I wrote. I wrote. And I wrote some more. It took well over a year to finish, and came out to 27,000 words. I finally sent the manuscript to George, who told me he enjoyed it, but that the magazine had been canceled, and he was no longer buying stories for it. I asked him if it was suitable for IASFM. (Which is still publishing, though George passed on in 2010.) Too long, he said, but asked me for shorter works. I sent *Firejammer* to all the other SF magazines, all of which rejected it because of its length. So I set it aside and went back to writing shorter fiction for IASFM.

Firejammer, by chance, had come out at what I began to call "that hideous length;" too long for the magazines and too short to publish as a novel. Come the 80s I had begun writing nonfiction for technical magazines like *Creative Computing*, and making a great deal more money at it. By 1984 I had stopped writing SF altogether, in favor of computer books like *Complete Turbo Pascal* and *Assembly Language Step By Step*. I didn't return to SF until the midlate 1990s. *Firejammer* was still the wrong size, and still in a box.

Once indie publishing became a possibility, I realized I could publish *Firejammer* (or anything else) irrespective of length. So in 2015 I pulled the tale out of the box, looked at it, and realized that it was conceived and written by a *much* younger me. I rewrote it, almost from scratch, carving out 2,500 words and nuking most of the 70s cultural references. (I left a couple in, for the fun of it. Did you find them?) It was a low-priority project. Larger things like *Ten Gentle Opportunities* got the lion's share of my time.

I realized during the rewrite that the style was familiar. Of course it was; in high school Keith Laumer was by far my favorite SF writer. I learned how to write SF by imitating the stories I enjoyed reading, and most of what I enjoyed reading was SF by Keith Laumer. Goofy aliens, incompetent bureaucrats, unlikely plots, the works. For all the SF giants I've met in my life, Keith Laumer was not among them, and he died in 1993. In many ways this story is a tribute to him, because he taught me how to write lighthearted stories with funny aliens.

Now here we are, in 2019, and the story that came to me in 1968, was written in 1979, and sat in a box until 2015 finally has its day in the marketplace. My beta readers loved it. Which leads me to wonder: What *else* might be in that box? I'm going to go take another look.

--Jeff Duntemann
Scottsdale, Arizona
May 1, 2019

ABOUT THE AUTHOR

Jeff Duntemann has written professionally since 1974, in both science fiction/fantasy and technical nonfiction. His early work in both areas reflects his experience as a programmer for Xerox in the 1970s and 1980s. His stories have appeared in *Isaac Asimov's Science Fiction Magazine*, *Omni*, the *Orbit* and *Nova* anthology series, and several standalone print anthologies. Two of his short stories have appeared on the final Hugo Awards ballot.

On the nonfiction side, he has worked as a technical editor for Ziff-Davis Publishing and Borland International, launched and edited two print magazines for programmers, and has twenty technical books to his credit, including the bestselling *Assembly Language Step By Step*. He wrote the "Structured Programming" column in *Dr. Dobb's Journal* for four years, and published technical articles in many magazines. He co-founded and ran editorial for The Coriolis Group, which became Arizona's largest book publisher in 1998.

After retiring from technical publishing, Jeff resumed his career as an indie SF author. Most of his fiction involves strong AI. His first novel, *The Cunning Blood*, appeared in hardcover from ISFiC Press in 2005. All his subsequent titles are available through Kindle, in both ebook and print editions. Outside of writing and publishing, Jeff's interests include programming, electronics, amateur radio (callsign K7JPD), telescopes, history, psychology, and kites. Jeff lives in Scottsdale, Arizona with his wife Carol and several bichon frise dogs.

Hard SF Action-Adventure at Its Best

Framed for murder by Eath's world government, Peter Novilio is offered his freedom in exchange for a reconnaisance mission to the surface of Hell, Earth's escape-proof prison planet. Hell is infected with a nanobug that eats electrical conductors, making computation and spaceflight impossible. There is a way back, known only to his grim mission partner, Gayle Shreve.

But Peter has a secret too: In his bloodstream he carries the Sangruse Device, an outlawed nanotech AI of fearsome power, with its own reasons for visiting Hell. Peter soon realizes that he is a pawn in a covert war among Earth, Hell's ingenious inmates, and the deadly mechanism in his veins. For as fearsome as it is, the Sangruse Device itself is afraid—and the fates of whole worlds would depend on the threat that the Cunning Blood had discovered outside of space and time.

See Amazon for both ebook and trade paperback formats

"[Jeff Duntemann] returns with an ambitious, polished tale of intrigue, nano-technology, and something that sounds a lot like mysticism...This one has a decent chance of ending up on award ballots." —Tom Easton, *Analog*

"The book is absolutely *au courant*, and actually extends the Great Work of SF in several unexpected directions. Like most ambitiously sprawling *sui generis* books, this one delivers the sense—as with the work of the recently departed Charles Harness—that the author has chucked every idea he had during the writing of the novel into the pot."   —Paul Di Filippo, *Science Fiction Weekly*

"Whether your interest is in scientific ideas, widescreen action, or sheer flights of imagination, you will find much to enjoy in *The Cunning Blood*. I look forward eagerly to Duntemann's future work." —David Hebblethwaite, *SFSite*

For More SF in the Grand Tradition...

...pick up *Cold Hands and Other Stories*, the newest collection of Jeff Duntemann's short SF and fantasy. This volume includes Jeff's first published story ("Our Lady of the Endless Sky") and the Hugo-nominated "Cold Hands." Three stories take place on Valinor, the Drumlins World: "Drumlin Boiler," "Drumlin Wheel," and "Roddie." As a bonus, there's a new excerpt from *The Cunning Blood*, Jeff's rollicking hard SF action saga of nanotech AI, and a break-out from a prison planet where a bacteria-sized nanotech bug prevents all things electronic from working. Don't miss it!

In This Volume:

- "Cold Hands"   *Nominated for the Hugo Award*
- "Our Lady of the Endless Sky"
- "Inevitability Sphere"
- "Whale Meat"
- "Born Again, with Water"
- "Drumlin Boiler"
- "Drumlin Wheel"
- "Roddie"
- ...and a new excerpt from his novel *The Cunning Blood*

"These stories convey a warmth and generosity of spirit, and an enthusiastic embrace of technology as a means to improve upon the best of mankind."
--Jon Mollison, Castalia House blog

"All told, a rich collection of short stories that you'd expect to be the work of half a dozen authors. A wide range of ideas, varying styles, varying outlooks on the universe...Highly recommended. --Goodreads

Magic and Monsters Vs. Software and AIs

Having cheated a magician out of ten nuggets of pure magic in a rigged card game, spellbender Bartholomew Stypek needs a place to hide. With his anarchic familiar spirit Pickles and the ill-won magical Opportunities, Stypek leaps blindly across universes, hoping to be dropped someplace far away and without magic... and lands in the break room of a small advertising agency in Upstate New York.

Because our universe doesn't support spirits, Pickles manifests as the local equivalent: AI software in the agency's heavily networked copier. She wanders into a nearby corporate network looking for allies, and finds a virtual universe where AIs live and train for jobs as AI products. Stypek, mistaken for a penniless CS intern, is taken in by the ad agency's copywriter. Expecting the usual suspicion and contempt, he is humbled by the kindness he's shown, and one by one uses the stolen Opportunities to help his new friends with their problems.

But Jrikk the magician isn't so easily thwarted. Soon Stypek, Pickles, and both their human and virtual friends must fight for their lives against the evil force sent to retrieve Stypek to the magician's dungeons.

Kindle EBook $2.99 Trade Paperback $12.99

"*Ten Gentle Opportunities* represents the best that science fiction and fantasy have to offer. It blends the two genres in a clever and original way. It presents near future tech that is plausible, delightful, and a little scary. Best of all, it provides an exuberant and unapologetic adventure that incorporates action, violence, romance, and robots in ways that are both exciting, fun to read, and even a little bit educational."

—Jon Mollison, Seagull Rising

Two Short Novels of the Drumlins World In One Volume

Step up to the pillars in front of the big bowl of gray dust, tap the pillars 256 times in any pattern, and *something* appears in the bowl. What? *Almost anything.* This is the Drumlins World, an alien planet where the aliens have gone, leaving their replicator machines behind, still working, still capable of producing 10^{77} different things—one for every atom in the universe! Here are two short novels by Drumlins creator Jeff Duntemann and *Brass and Steel* author Jim Strickland:

• In *Drumlin Circus*, a circus master attempts to free his wife from the shadowy Bitspace Institute, with the help of his bodyguard clowns (one a former Institute man with a grudge against the organization) and a preteen girl with a whistle drumlin that can make other drumlins, animals, and even human beings obey her. Intrigue, steam, smilodons, airships, and nonstop action!

• *On Gossamer Wings* tells the story of a teen girl who cannot speak, but has a strange talent allowing her to find exactly the drumlin she wants among the 10^{77} possibilities in the Thingmakers. Her farm town neighbors hold her in contempt, and she struggles to realize her dream of building a drumlin flying machine before the Bitspace Institute fully comprehends the breadth of her powers.

Kindle EBook $2.99 Trade Paperback $12.99